SEEP

ALSO BY W. MARK GILES
Knucklehead & Other Stories

W. MARK GILES

SEEP

(A Novel)

ANVIL PRESS / VANCOUVER

Library and Archives Canada Cataloguing in Publication

Giles, W. Mark, author
     Seep / W. Mark Giles.

ISBN 978-1-77214-012-5 (paperback)

    I. Title.

PS8563.I47637S44 2015   C813'.6   C2015-904152-X

Printed and bound in Canada
Cover design by Rayola Graphic
Interior by HeimatHouse
Represented in Canada by the Publishers Group Canada
Distributed by Raincoast Books

Anvil Press Publishers Inc.
P.O. Box 3008, Main Post Office
Vancouver, B.C. V6B 3X5 CANADA
www.anvilpress.com

The publisher gratefully acknowledges the financial assistance of the Canada Council for the Arts, the Government of Canada through the Canada Book Fund, and the Province of British Columbia through the B.C. Arts Council and the Book Publishing Tax Credit.

Only connect! That was the whole of her sermon. Only connect the prose and the passion, and both will be exalted, and human love will be seen at its height.

—E.M. Forster, *Howard's End*

Connect nothing: F shouted. Place things side by side on your arborite table, if you must, but connect nothing!

— Leonard Cohen, *Beautiful Losers*

Once Upon a Time

Once upon a time, "once upon a time" was a good way to start a story. Indeed, "once upon a time" was a sly beginning, archaic, ambiguous, redundant. "Once upon a time" concealed its slyness with its familiarity, like the handshake of a freemason. "Once upon a time" let the listener of a story know that whatever followed was safely distant — it affirmed a sense of "that was then and this now," and — more to the point — "we know better than that now." "Once upon a time" reminded everyone to appreciate the newness of the now (and the nowness of the new), the presence of the present — even as it made stories of the past all the more delicious because of the pastness of the then (and the thenness of the past).

Who tells a story? Of course, we all do, all the time, filling our heads with one "once upon a time" after another, dreaming the stories of ourselves. But everyone knows a storyteller. The one we turn to during the contemplative lull around the fire, while holding each other for warmth against the cold and the dark, in the car or train or bus on a long trip, sitting on the stoop on a hot summer night. We turn and we say, Tell me a story. The best storytellers — or at least the ones that appeal the most — don't immediately resort to self-important and dramatic flourishes. They don't wave their hands in the air, they don't jump around, they don't talk in funny voices, then suddenly shout at the top of their lungs like they're trying to get the attention of six-year-olds.

We're not six-year-olds. The best storytellers leave all that mimicry and shouting and jumping to the imaginations of the listeners.

But wait a minute. We *are* all six years old. The confounding slyness of "once upon a time" lets us remember six or sixteen or twenty-six at sixty-six. To utter "once upon a time" is to create a time machine — erasing distance even as the utterance establishes it, transforming the then-time of story into the now-time of telling.

How was this notice in a newspaper a way of saying "once upon a time"?

OPEN HOUSE
PUBLIC MEETING
SEEP SITE PROPOSED DEVELOPMENT
LAND USE STRUCTURE PLAN
MUNICIPAL DISTRICT OF SHEEPSHORN NO. 19

The notice stated that the project in question was a "proposed development" — but in fact this was a *re*development. Before it was ever known as "Seep" to European explorers and surveyors, the land at Seep had had uses for thousands of years — millions of years of geologic use. The notice begins to tell a story: Once upon a time this place served other, lesser purposes, but now we are going to build a shiny, smartly designed and thoughtfully planned community for six thousand financially qualified and responsibly minded people. How else could this story begin: with a house in the road.

0.

"Amy's" Prelude

22 August 2009

I get the first word. I'll get the last word, too, but that comes later. At the end. I found these pages in a box he left in Boadicea's house. Boadicea is my dog. That's her real name. She has to sleep in a dog house. I can't take her in the crew trailer. His name really isn't "Dwight." My name isn't "Amy." There isn't a town called "Seep." But I know — knew? — a man a lot like "Dwight." We grew up in a place that I recognize as "Seep," however different it is the from the way he tells it. "Dwight" had an older brother. I slept with him. The brother that is. Often. For a while. We were both young and stupid. Well, he was stupid, I was just young. He's the father of my daughter, "Willow." That brother wasn't named "Darcy," but his name did start with the same letter as "Dwight."

He writes about himself in the third person, like he exists outside of himself. I suppose this character "Dwight" isn't exactly like him, so maybe he's not writing about himself, exactly. But kind of. I never got that about some people — those who address themselves in third person. Hockey players always do it. The man I know (knew?) isn't exactly the "Dwight" in these pages, nor am I exactly the "Amy." "Willow" says that the way he adopts "he" as a narrator is like the "I" writing an "I" who is not the being-I. I just copied that from a sticky-note she gave me, because I told her I'd never remember it. I guess you can say stuff like

9

that when you have more than one university degree, like my "Willow" does. I almost get it. Ai-Ai. Aye-Aye. Eye for an eye. The seeing eye. The being-I.

So I'll be back at the end, for the last word. I'll wait till then to set a few facts straight — or maybe it's setting a few fictions straight. I was going to list them all out here, but "Willow" says not to. Spoilers, she calls them. But now, like the man says, Once upon a time . . .

Dear Dwight—

All these years you have been asking me about the day you were born, about your father, and all these years I have not answered. Yes it is painful but not in the way you think it is. Now you are mixed up in some scheme to do something there in Seep, save the town? Just what is there left to save? I know you have an idea that your memory and sense of family and who you are, somehow it's all mixed up in that place and I guess of all of us — you, Darcy, Lance, me — you have the most reason, you were born there and we stuck you with that crazy story about the baseball game.

1.

All the Cars He Had Ever Owned

10-11 May 2009

Dwight Eliot was driving a car imagining a man driving a car. The man he imagined bore a resemblance to Dwight, but he was younger; he was also older. His car was newer; it was also older. Dwight's imagined man was not *a* man, but all the men that Dwight had been or could be, all at the same time. The imagined man was not driving *a* car, but all the cars Dwight had ever owned. A '63 Fairlane with a cracked head. A '50 Studebaker pickup truck painted with house paint. '72 Mazda 808 station wagon. Another '72 Mazda 808 station wagon bought with the insurance money from the first wreck. '55 Fairlane with a Ford-o-matic three speed (skidded into a light-pole on drizzly pavement). '74 Jeep half-ton (dropped into a frame-bending ditch on a run through a construction site in the dark). '80 vw van. '68 Meteor Montcalm (towed to and never claimed from the impound lot). '70 BMW 2002 (the funnest car he ever owned). '72 Honda Civic donated to the Kidney Foundation. '83 Mazda GLC run to four hundred thousand clicks. '66 Plymouth Valiant Signet with a 225 slant-six that wouldn't quit. '78 vw van. '95 Toyota Corolla. '92 Oldsmobile Ciera (the shortest ownership, T-boned by a speeding Laredo after nine days insured). '87 Chevrolet Cavalier station wagon (easily the worst car ever, also donated to the Kidney Foundation). '97 Toyota Corolla.

The man who was all the men Dwight had ever been or could be was driving all the cars that Dwight had ever owned on all the roads that

Dwight had ever driven. Dwight imagined this as he drove his '97 Corolla north on Highway 22 in Alberta, Canada, just short of the wide turn at the head of the Waldron Community Pasture, approaching the sweep of hill that would take him up and over into the Willow Creek watershed. Dwight imagined the man behind the wheel of a subset of all the cars he had ever owned — a subset equal to those cars that he had actually driven up the sweep of hill at the head of the Waldron: the '97 Corolla, the '95 Corolla, the '78 vw, the Valiant, the Mazda GLC, the '80 vw, the BMW 2002, the Jeep, the first Mazda 808 station wagon.

Dwight was driving at dawn on a day in late May. The sky was clear. The sun had just begun to glance above the Porcupine Hills to the east. The imagined man drove all the cars that Dwight had ever owned, and the subset of all the cars he had ever driven up the sweep of hill at Waldron's head, through all the weather that Dwight had ever encountered on Highway 22. The August snowstorm when the wipers on the '78 vw van stopped working, the rainstorm in the Mazda 808 that pounded water through the windshield seal, the hundred-degree July day that boiled the radiator in the Jeep half-ton dry, the cracking cold December night when the gasoline heater in the '80 vw van failed and the oil warning light came on and his brother Darcy and he had to make it to the Calgary airport for an early morning flight and they asked themselves: is the oil warning light on because the oil pump is broken or a seal is blown or a cylinder is cracked or is the oil light on because when it's this cold the instrumentation on a '80 vw van does unpredictable things and maybe the oil pressure sender switch has frozen. After all, hadn't the heater frozen up? And if we keep driving will the motor seize and strand us here, or do we stop driving and strand ourselves? They had not seen another vehicle since they turned off from the Crowsnest Pass highway. And they asked themselves these questions with a handful of words — Oil light come on. Pause. Oil pump? Pause. Blown seal. Pause. Sender switch? — and they came to the decision that it was too cold to stop the van and check the oil level or look for leaks, the tools were frozen and under a pile of gear, there were no cars on the road to flag down (this was in the days before cellular phones). Dwight was younger then, younger than the imaginary man driving all his cars, and without saying a word they made the decision not to stop, they drove on, the decision not so much arrived at as it was enacted, and they drove with the red light illuminating an iconographic silhouette of an oil can eking out its last drop. They were bundled in parkas, wrapped in scarves in the heaterless van. Dwight's fingers were numb in his down-filled mittens. His feet were turning cold inside army surplus snow boots that were so big he could barely depress the accelerator without also engaging the brake pedal. His wolverine-fur fringed hood was pulled around his face. No peripheral vision. The side windows were opaque with frost anyways. He hunched over the oversized vw steering wheel, peering through his fur portal and out through the ragged square foot of windscreen that his brother kept polishing with the long-handled ice scraper, peeling ribbons of frost from the glass that collected on the dashboard like dropped threads and dust. The two brothers listened to the thrum of the engine through muffles of hood and tuque and scarf, wondering. It was too cold to talk, but they listened, poorly as they could, waiting for the knock of a main bearing run dry, the explosion of piston separating from a red-hot connecting rod, the rattle of thirsty valves shattering like icicles knocked from an eave. Nearly deaf and blind, they drove that van up the sweep of hill at the head of the Waldron in the glow of the oil light in the cold black before dawn on a December night where the mercury found the bulb at the bottom of thermometers. And they couldn't see the Chinook arch that stretched in the dark over the Front Range to the west, pushing the mass of warm air towards them, but Dwight could feel the west wind as it slammed the boxy vw van broadside until they were drifting from shoulder to yellow line to shoulder as he steered and over-steered against the gusts and the temperature rose forty degrees Celsius in ten kilometres and the oil light went out and the gasoline heater kicked in and the narrative of enthalpy told the threads of frost on the dashboard to evaporate and condense again as moisture on the windshield. By the time they got to Chain Lakes they had stripped off their parkas and hats, and Dwight's fingers burned on the steering wheel as they warmed. Darcy snapped open a can of frozen Coca-Cola for Dwight and a can of Labatt's 50 Ale for himself and the motor thrummed on. Sender switch, he said and raised his can like he was offering a toast. Sender switch, Dwight said.

Dwight was driving the '97 Corolla towards the sweep of hill at the head of the Waldron on a crepuscular May morning, imagining a man and all the cars, remembering the oil light in the '80 vw van, when around the bend ahead of him a pilot vehicle approached. WIDE LOAD. Dwight traced his eyes up the and around the curve. He saw a house. The highway just before the curve was narrow. The swale of hills that run into the Whaleback rose abruptly to the west. The broad dish of valley with its meandering creek sloped away to the east. The roadway was built on an embankment between this high and that low, with sharp shoulders. Dwight spotted a grassy berm ahead to the right, where the road widened a bit to create an access point to the pasture. He pulled over and waited.

The sun rose higher. The light was the clear gold of the photographer's magic hour. The house crept towards him, growing larger, and turning from a grey shadow to a clear white. He rolled down his window. Meadow smells. Cows in the middle distance to his right occasionally mooed. Dwight thought about all the houses he had ever lived in. He imagined all the families he had ever had simultaneously living in all the houses. Father, mother, brother. Wives and a near-wife. Long-absent children. Homes, not just houses, homes. Apartments. Some hotel rooms. A residence at university. He thought that the house coming down the road at what seemed like a walking pace reminded him of the house where he grew up, in Seep, except it was on a highway, jacked up on timbers, being towed behind a truck. Instead of windows, it had particleboard nailed over the openings. He looked, and he thought, other than the fact that it's on timbers behind a truck with boarded windows, it looks identical to my house in Seep.

It was close enough now to see where the paint had peeled in great chunks, exposing the grey weathered siding. The asphalt shingles were buckling in spots, but were for the most part intact. It was the same pale green he remembered from boyhood, with a four-foot edging of tin at the eaves to encourage the snow to shed. Behind one of the boarded windows would be the dining room, and behind the other, the kitchen. The window in the half-storey above would be the room he shared with Darcy.

As the house passed, Dwight looked at the long side of what he knew to be the back of the house. And there it was — or wasn't. To the left of the back door, about three feet up from the level of the sill and two feet from the jamb, a strip of shiplap siding was missing — not the whole piece, but the bottom half, peeled off in a scimitar shape. Dwight thought, that is mine. That missing half-strip of shiplap is mine. I did that. He had prised it off with a hatchet when he was ten years old. If you send a ten-year-old into the yard, to get him out from underfoot, to where the boards on the siding of the house have dried and split, and he discovers his older brother has left a hatchet buried in a stump, this is the result.

My house, Dwight thinks. My shiplap autograph. The house moved away behind him, getting smaller in his rearview mirror, further away from where he sat in his '97 Corolla, parked on the side of the road. The sweep of hill at the head of the Waldron loomed before him. Dwight didn't go to work in Calgary that Monday. When he got to 22X he swung left instead of right.

I think families often make happy stories to hide the shitty things that are really happening. Your story took hold of you from the first moment, and there was nothing I could do to stop it. And I suppose a kind of legend about the day you are born is bound to happen when that day has so much hullabaloo about it. But I never went in for that too much, fake happy stories, or storytelling at all, and as you were never shy of telling me, I never really wanted to talk about the past even when I still had my voicebox and yes it's true that not talking has been a kind of blessing for me, if it's possible to find a blessing or anything good from a disease that steals the lower half of your face. I suppose if I were religious, blessing might be the word I would use, "the lord works in mysterious ways" and all that, but as you know well, religion and faith were never too strong in our household and no amount of visits from well-meaning zealots or sincere heart-to-heart chats with my god-fearing and Jesus-loving fellow residents here at Crumbly Bricks Home for the Aged and Decrepit have changed that.

2.

Amy Among the Earthmovers

11 May 2009

Dwight didn't actually have a "work" to go to. The Wednesday previous he'd been made redundant. Laid off. Downsized. Outsourced. Terminated. Fired from his job as archivist in the corporate library of IHC — Integrated Horizons Corp, formerly International Hydrocarbons, formerly Industrial Heat & Coal, originally Prairie Mountain Light & Power. He didn't have work, but today was to have been his first day with PeopleFirst! PeopleFirst! was where they sent you after they fire you, where you received transition counselling, and partook in career planning, and networked with your peers who didn't have jobs. I feel like I've finally arrived, he explained to his mother the day before. This is the first time I've been let go where they gave me money to go away, and outplacement support. I've arrived. I hit the middle management bingo.

Don't be ridiculous, Dwight's mother wrote on her notepad. She abbreviated ridiculous as ridic. You got $$ before when fired. She tore off the small square of paper and handed it to him. Dwight made a point of visiting her every second Sunday, driving down to Coleman where she lived in the Crowsnest Pass Regional Long-Term Care facility. This Sunday was Mother's Day. He brought her a pad of premium watercolour paper, and some paints that he knew she could always use — zinc white, cerulean blue, burnt sienna. And a stack of scratch 'n' win BigBingo lottery tickets.

His mother didn't have a tongue, nor a jawbone on her right side, nor a larynx. She breathed through a hole in her throat. She could have had a synthetic voicebox installed, but she preferred to write notes. Dwight also brought her a steady supply of 3x5 coil notebooks that he picked up by the dozen at a dollar store. She wrote more notes without a voice than she used to speak with one. She was eighty years old and she liked to sit in the lodge's lounge and paint what she could see from her window. She wrote something else and handed it to Dwight. It was one word: Darcy.

Have I talked to Darcy, Dwight said.

She shook her head, and pointed to her own chest. Darcy called you. She nodded. Why, he asked. She shrugged. Did he ask you for money? She shook her head, but Dwight knew she was lying. Did you send him some? She shook her head, and this time was telling the truth. That's something. He's using again, Dwight said, but his mother didn't respond. She was furiously writing. You didn't give him my phone number, did you? Did you talk about me? She kept writing. I don't want him to know I'm out of work, Dwight said. Sometimes she didn't hand over her notes, just tore them off the pad and stuffed them in her pocket. She did that now.

Are you going to scratch those tickets, he said. I can do it for you.

His mother passed a copy of the *East Slope News* and tapped the notice about the Seep townsite development. Once upon a time.

On the morning he was all the men he ever was or could be, driving all the cars he had ever owned up Highway 22, where he encountered his house on the road, the day after his mother had showed him the newspaper notice about the redevelopment of the townsite where he had been born on a baseball diamond, Dwight turned left instead of right when he came to the junction of 22X. He turned away from his scheduled intake meeting at PeopleFirst! and his not-job at IHC in the city, and headed for Seep. He passed around the big loop that enclosed the farm with goats and llamas and miniature donkeys, through Bragg Creek, then west again on the Trans-Canada, through the rolling prairie broken by the Jumping Pound Ridge and the hill at Scott Lake. The casino on reserve land near the Seep turnoff was finally open. Newest in Alberta, its sign proclaimed. Loose Slots!

A half hour later Dwight stood on what was left of the pitcher's mound on the Seep baseball diamond. In left field, earthmoving equipment sat idle: two scrapers, a bulldozer, buckets, hydraulic picks and other components for the two shovels he had seen busily knocking down buildings and trees elsewhere in town. A prefab trailer that served as the site office occupied centre field. Further along the road, out of sight of the field, three ATCO dormitory trailers perched near where the General Store used to be. Crew camp. A four-door four-wheel-drive pickup pulled into the rough patch of mud that served as a parking area in right field and stopped beside where he had left his Toyota. A woman hopped down from the driver's side, followed by a bounding, woolly-haired dog. She moved and stood behind Dwight's car. She wore a black nylon jacket with the blaze of a patch on the shoulder. She talked into a handheld device — a cellphone or radio. She was calling in his licence tag.

Dwight held a stick in his right hand, a board he had picked up behind what remained of the backstop. Maybe a piece of a seat slat from the bleachers that had once been there. It was longer than the shiplap strip he had once peeled from the siding of his house, that he had held in his hand forty years earlier in this same spot, where fifty years earlier he had been born. It was wider too. The dog forty years ago had been small, a terrier. He turned his back on the security guard and walked toward where he imagined home plate should be, stepping over the lumpy tussocks of weeds and grass. He hopped through the chassis of a rusted-out car or truck — nothing left of the body, only the frame and a knuckle of a flathead engine block. He used the board to beat through the shrubs of wild rose and dogwood, until he reached a scrub

23

of aspens that had colonized the area behind home, where the catcher and the umpire would crouch. They were young aspens still, half again as high as he was, and they stretched toward the first baseline and the home team dugout. The remnant of the dugout itself was little more than a trench, filled with a ragged hedge of willows that had taken root in the low spot where moisture gathered. He turned and faced the outfield. He gripped the board like a bat, but awkwardly. The wood was flat, a 5/4 x 5 piece of decking, and long as a spade. He swung it a couple of times, swatting imaginary balls towards where the fence might have been.

The woman and the dog began walking towards him. The dog arrived first, bouncing over the uneven ground, slowing to a trot as it came close. The dog was hip-high, tawny, curly, with a head the size and shape of a good-sized butternut squash. Dwight was wary, but he clocked the wagging tail, the forward-cocked ears, the springy, confident gait. He let his hands fall to his sides, and rested the tip of the stick on the ground. The dog circled two or three times, nuzzled his free hand, sniffed quickly at his crotch, then bowed in front of him in a posture of play. Without really thinking, Dwight tossed the stick. It helicoptered a third of the way toward first. The dog barked twice and went after it. It gripped the board at one end and struggled to carry it back, dropping it and picking it up repeatedly as it caught in the brush and knocked against the slender trunks of the aspens. The dog dropped the stick at his feet. He tossed it again. This time the dog didn't fetch it back, but settled down to gnaw at it.

The woman was now only a couple of dozen paces from him. She spoke first. Hi Dwight, she said. Long time no see. Or maybe, she said, Long time no Seep.

Hi Amy, Dwight said.

What brings you here, she said.

He shrugged. Old times' sake, he said. Wanted to have a look at the hole where my house used to be. They stood there for a while. Dwight broke from Amy's gaze and looked past her to where the slab of the Rockies rose into the first of the mountains. The dog came over so Amy could scratch its neck.

Nice dog, Dwight said. You always had a dog. He remembered a terrier. What is he? Dwight said.

She, Amy said, She's a Labradoodle.

Dwight looked at Amy and raised an eyebrow. A Labradoodle?

Yeah. Part Labrador. Part poodle, she said. Standardbred poodle.

I know what a Labradoodle is. But I figured you for a Heinz 57 type. Or maybe a rescued greyhound. But not a Labradoodle. I never figured you for a designer dog.

Now it was Amy's turn to look away, in the other direction, where behind the trees the prairie began its thousand-mile stretch. Had me figured, eh? she said. I wondered when you'd show up here again. The scene of the crime so to speak.

What crime? Who said anything about a crime? Dwight said.

It's a figure of speech, Amy said. The crime of your birth. She tossed her head in the direction of third base. Dwight's mother had gone into labour under the grandstand; he had been born near the visitors' dugout.

Yeah, Dwight said. I should have been a natural. I hate baseball. Stupid game.

You gotta go, Amy said. No unauthorized personnel on the development site.

That's what I like about you, Amy, he said. I don't see you for five years and we just pick up where we left off.

Ten.

Ten what?

Ten years, she said. You show up every ten years like a plague of locusts.

Locusts come every seven years. Or maybe fourteen.

Whatever. You gotta go. They're touchy about visitors.

They? he said. Who are they?

25

Amy shrugged. Some bigwigs from Calgary. Or maybe the States. And the band.

The band is in on all this?

Yeah, Amy said. They're forty-nine point nine percent partners. It's freehold land. Not reserve.

Dwight was shaking his head, as if he was bewildered. The First Nations band wants to build a resort town here? They bought back the land that was taken from them so they could build condos for white people?

Whatever, Amy said. You gotta go. They think everyone's a troublemaker.

Like some sort of earth-liberation terrorist?

Maybe. Maybe an unhappy band member. Or maybe a long-lost townie who's mad at the holes in the ground, Amy said. C'mon. She turned towards the vehicles in right centre. They began to pick their way across the overgrown field. The dog picked up the board and carried it ahead of them. Then she dropped it to trade it for a smaller stick.

Forty years, Dwight said. A plague of locusts every forty years.

Well, Amy said, you show up every ten.

The sun was high and hot in the way the sun can be in the spring, promising summer to come. A few crocuses were still in bloom under foot. A jay squawked. Just at the limits of their hearing was the roar of the rush of water over the spillway of the dam on the river. The river and the dam divided Seep — on this side was what they always called the company town, or New Seep, the few hundred acres carved out of the Indian reserve a hundred years ago. The company town was built to service this dam and the other one a half-mile downriver. They were run-of-river dams, holding back modest reservoirs, but relying on the natural forces of water volume and gravity. New Seep housed the workers, the control room operators, the maintenance shifts, the travelling crews of linemen, and the teachers, doctors, nurses, barbers, storekeeps, bartenders, Chinese laundrymen and others that the Industrial Heat & Coal recruited.

For a few years after the war they even had a coal tip here, loading trains with soft coal that Industrial Heat & Coal hauled to the railhead from a dig a few miles up a side valley, and the miners swelled New Seep's population into the hundreds. On the other side of the river was what they called real Seep, or Old Seep, the hamlet that had been established when the railroad built the last station on the prairies at the foot of the Seep escarpment, with a grain elevator and a bank and a one-room school for those homesteaders who filled the last acres of arable land before the mountains. Old Seep had been dwindling since it was founded. Its grain elevator was one of the first to close. Dwight grew up in New Seep, Amy in both New and Old Seep.

How's Willow keeping these days, Dwight said. I haven't seen her since, I don't know, maybe she was in grade four or something.

If he had been looking at her, Dwight would have seen Amy's face soften, noticed how her chin seemed to lift, how her eyes seemed to suddenly find a bright spot in the horizon. But he kept his head down, watching the broken ground. She's great, Amy said. Almost thirty. Got two university degrees. Travelled all over the world. Africa. India. France. She's in Malcolm now. Malcolm was a bigger town just upriver. The last town on the highway before the national park, Malcolm was booming as a recreational destination. The other way, downriver away from the mountains, the town of Caxton was becoming a bedroom community for the city.

She's fierce, Amy said.

Like her mom, Dwight said, and Amy laughed sharply, as if she was both contemptuous of the flattery, but also pleased.

Fiercer, Amy said. She's part of a group that's trying to stop all this.

This?

All this, she said, gesturing in a way that took in the ball diamond, the heavy equipment, the ATCO trailers where the General Store used to be, the sound of the backhoes just out of sight that were chewing through the houses in Seep that were too rundown to hoist onto beams and move behind trucks down Highway 22 and the sweep of the hill at the head of the Waldron community pasture.

Is she a terrorist? Or a long-lost townie? Dwight said.

Amy shook her head. Just some people who say the valley can't sustain another resort town, she said.

What do you say?

Amy allowed frustration into her voice. Always the questions from you. Dwight the interrogator.

So Willow's fighting these bastards and her mother's a rent-a-cop for them. Go figure.

Yeah, go figure, Dwight. They walked. Suddenly the dog stopped short and flattened her ears. She let out a low growl. They were almost at the vehicles. A coyote stepped from behind the office trailer and stared frankly at the humans and the dog. The dog broke for the coyote, barking wildly, but she had too much ground to make up. The coyote turned and loped off between the bulldozer and an earth scraper, and disappeared.

Boadicea, Amy called after the dog. Boadicea, come. The dog slowed, then stopped, hesitating, torn between the command and the desire to pursue her quarry. She returned to Amy, but now she was alert, agitated, still growling.

Dwight was smirking. Boadicea? Your dog's name is Boadicea? You named your Labradoodle Boadicea?

They were beside Dwight's Toyota. Amy turned quickly to face him and shoved him with both her hands on his chest. Dwight stumbled backwards a couple of paces. He tripped on a knot of foxtail grasses and thistles and fell on his ass.

Oh fuck off, Amy said. You fuck off, Dwight Eliot. Who do you think you are, you fucking locust. You show up here with your fucking sarcasm. You figure this, you figure that, like you figure you have a fucking right to figure anything you want. Your house is gone. Oh boohoo. You can just waltz in here and cluck your tongue. Like you still have some sort of claim to something. You were born here. You're some fucking legend because you were born in a baseball game. B.F.D. Big fucking deal. BF fucking D. Other people were from here too, some of us stayed, we fucking well stayed. You can just fuck off. Oh my, Amy's a rent-a-cop and her dog is so funny, it's all so fucking ironic. Fuck you, you don't know me, you can't figure me like some fucking game. I'm not a game. I'm fifty fucking years old just like you, you fucking locust. I'm a security guard, OK? I gotta pay the bills like anybody else. What the fuck else is a fifty-year-old half-breed orphan single mother supposed to do. Get in your fucking car and go back to your sarcastic figuring life and come back in another ten years.

All the time she was talking, Amy paced three or four steps this way and that, speaking to the sky and the mountains and the prairie, but with the last word she stopped and stared hard at Dwight who was still sitting on the ground. Boadicea was running to and fro beside Amy, barking, but she stopped too. Her ears were pinned back, and she snarled. As Dwight began to pick himself up, avoiding the thistles, the dog lunged a half-step forward and bared her teeth.

Easy now, Dwight said, looking at the dog, then at Amy, then at the dog again.

Bodie, come, Amy said. The dog moved to her side. Sit. The dog obeyed. Amy grabbed Boadicea by the collar. Get up, she said.

Dwight got to his feet and dusted himself off. The ass of his khaki pants was wet. He had a streak of mud on his jaw. They looked at each other. Jesus Christ, he said. Jesus Christ, Amy. What the hell is going on. Maybe this town was a pile of shit, but what they're doing here is a bigger pile of shit. Dwight wiped his face with the back of his hand, then dug his car keys out of his pocket.

I saw my house on Highway 22 this morning. Being towed by a truck, Dwight said. I came to look at the divot in the ground where they dug it up like a weed. And all the other divots where other houses used to be. The general store where I used to buy pop — where *we* used

29

to buy pop. Remember how you and me and Darcy would buy those bottles of warm Canada Dry ginger beer? Not the ginger ale, the ginger beer, fucking dark and spicy ginger beer. And warm. Not from the cooler, from the shelf. And we'd take turns swigging it, feeling the burn in the back of our throats and up our nose? The general store is a pile of kindling, with the goddamn ghouls living in trailers on top of it.

That's funny, Amy said.

What's so fucking funny. It's not funny.

It's funny because I'm one of the ghouls, Amy said. I'm squatting in one of those trailers right now. Comes with the job. Saves me rent.

Christ on a fucking crutch, Dwight said.

You gotta go, Dwight, Amy said. There's nothing left. It's too late.

Is that what Willow thinks? It's too late?

She's young. She still believes in possibilities.

I'm sorry, Dwight said. For what I said. For teasing.

Don't make it worse. I shouldn't have pushed you. You can be a jerk, you know that.

Dwight stood, and moved his mouth like he was starting to say something else, but then didn't. Amy turned away. She pulled a deck of smokes from a pocket of her jacket. She put her back to him and lit up. Boadicea had relaxed and was sniffing in a gopher hole nearby. Dwight got into his car and rolled down his window. Do you ever hear from Darcy, he said.

Amy grunted in a way that expressed deep loathing. Your brother's a bigger prick than you are.

He called my mom last week, Dwight said.

Amy looked over. How is she, she said.

My mom? I asked her that the other day, how are you. She wrote a note: every day I wake up is a good day. Thanks for asking.

She's good people, Amy said. No thanks to her boys.

I thought if Darcy called her, he might call you. You know how he operates. He hasn't ripped off any of us for a long while. We're due.

Dwight started the car. Can I call you sometime? I might come out here again.

You know where to find me, Amy said. I live in the end unit of one of the trailers. The one with the doghouse beside it.

Dwight fished a business card from his wallet. I'll give you my number. Can I borrow a pen?

Amy tossed her cigarette butt on the ground and twisted it with the toe of her boot. She pulled a pen from a small pocket on the sleeve of her jacket. Before she handed it to him, she wrote her own number on a piece of paper from her notebook, then passed the pen and paper to Dwight. He circled his cellphone number on his card, and wrote something on the back of it. You can reach me on my mobile. Don't have a landline. I put my email on the back. You have email, right?

Amy looked at the card and laughed. There's the pot calling the kettle black, she said. Corporate archivist for IHC? And you mock me for being a security guard? IHC sold your birthright down the river.

Give me that thing, Dwight said. He took the card and stroked through the corporate info and handed it back to her. I don't work there anymore. I got laid off last week.

That sucks, Amy said.

Dwight put the car in gear and inched forward. Take care of your dog. And Willow. And yourself.

You too, Amy said and Dwight drove off. Hey! she called after him. You took my pen, you bastard. But he didn't stop. Boadicea barked.

If anything, instead of God in our house in Seep we had the devil. It wasn't the Holy Spirit but the spirits that come in bottles. Ha ha. I don't believe in the devil any more than I believe a God. But I know the power of spirits. I know that is not a surprise to you, I know you remember the drinking or some of it and you've talked to all those old men in the town for whom Lance was some kind of combination of Superman and Errol Flynn — swashbuckler, doctor, fighter, lifesaver, skirt chaser, saint. You probably don't know who Errol Flynn was. But even as those old fogies play up Lance's sainthood, part of his legend is how he could put away the drink. Put any man under the table. Drank prodigiously, as they say. Like it's a talent. Dwight, have you ever wondered how it was we came to live in Seep in the first place? How it was that a man who had been in the top of his class at one of the most prestigious medical schools in the world ended up the company doctor? How someone who had been a war surgeon couldn't be trusted to suture a gash?

3.

Hot Shave

16 August 1959; June 1995-July 1999

The Roman writer Horace, in his treatise *Ars Poetica*, advised writers to begin a narrative *in medias res*, in the middle of things. Don't start the story *ab ovo*, from the egg. Homer's *Iliad* is no less compelling — indeed, maybe it is more compelling — because it begins in the eighth year of a ten-year war, and ends even before the famous horse is delivered to the gates of Troy.

But Dwight in the middle of an overgrown baseball diamond was both *in medias res* and *ab ovo*. As he played with a stick in the midst of the desolation of his hometown, he was inhabiting the very place of his birth. Just as when he drove Highway 22 in the rosy-fingered dawn he was all the men he had ever been and ever will be, and as he drove his Toyota he was driving all the cars he had ever owned, so too on the mound he was a man of fifty contemplating ruin at the same time he was a ten-year-old boy tormenting a dog with a shiplap scrap at the same time he was taking his first slap on the backside, gulping his first lungful of air, and squalling his first yawp. And when Amy reminded him it had been a decade since he had last been to Seep, she was reminding him too that the last occasion he spent time in Seep was to find the truth of the day of his birth. In August of 1959, during an annual tournament that bestowed $3,000 to the winning side, the Seep Selects took the field against a team of barnstorming Cubans. A riot broke out. He had been hearing about it all his life.

35

Whether it was the beanball delivered by Cody "Farmboy" Cody to the head of Luis "Sugarcane" Santiago, or the spiking by Sugarcane of the second baseman Ed Zosky, was a moot point, albeit one hotly debated. Uncle Alex, who was not really his uncle, swore by the former: I should know, he would say. I filed a story that was picked up across the wire. His father, who was (as far as he knew) really his father, held to the latter: After all, I was the attending physician.

Whatever events may have transpired that day in 1959 were obscured by time, by the vagaries of eyewitness subjectivity, by selective memory. Through the years Dwight had become the unquestioned authority on the matter — if in fact anyone can be an authority about a story for which there are as many versions as there are tellers. Not that he was present, exactly, the day it happened. His mother went into labour under the grandstand before the game began, and Dwight was born there, during negotiations to end the standoff — what Uncle Alex called the cowardly taking of a defenceless hostage, in the person of Beulah Howse. Uncle Alex, as was his custom, was guilty of stretching the truth in the interests of self-promotion. A Calgary newspaper was the only one, other than Alex's own, in which Dwight could ever find reference to the event — true enough, Alex got a byline, "Special Report to the Albertan," but that was hardly a wire-service leader. And neither there nor in his own *Sheepshorn Surveyor* were the events on the field leading up to the riot reported in much detail. From the Calgary *Albertan*:

Baseball Melee in Seep
Special to the Albertan
by Alexander Wiggins

A melee erupted in the fifth inning of an exhibition baseball game between a team of touring all-stars from Cuba and the Seep Selects at the annual Sheepshorn District Summer Fair this week past. Players from both teams required medical attention. According to RCMP constable James Peebles, charges are pending. The Cuban team is reported to have left the province, if not the country.

Uncle Alex's copy in his own weekly was more colourful, if not more forthcoming with the facts:

Cuban Infidels Riot in Seep!
Hostage Standoff Threat Thwarted as Cooler Heads Prevail

The happy celebration that was the Sheepshorn Summer Fair and Agricultural Exposition turned into an afternoon of South American Violence and Terror this past Saturday. A gang of marauding Cubans disguised as baseball players wreaked havoc through Seep in a display that would do the Revolutionary and Bandit Fidel Castro proud.

The day dawned fresh and clear, and all the town and half the county lined Main Street in Old Seep to witness the annual Summer Parade, led this year by Mountain Meadow Queen Patsy Potsma, resplendently robed in her golden gown, and attended by an even half-dozen white-frocked Wildflower Princesses. The festive mood of the crowd was buoyed by the procession of Malcolm Composite High School's Major Majorette Corps and Marching Band, conducted by the Musical Director, Seep's very own Horsham Newbigging. They were followed by the handsomely decorated bicycles of the 433rd Boy Scout Troop, who performed nifty precision drills under the command of

Scout Master Roland Blaines. Our dusky good neighbours were not unaccounted for, as Chief Roger Peacock led a passel of pinto ponies carrying braves and maidens bedecked in feathers and paint. The banter amongst the gentlefolk in attendance was full of glee and hope to match the temperament of this most perfect summer season.

As the happy revellers thronged to the fairgrounds in New Seep for an afternoon of cotton candy, carousel rides and livestock judging, none could have predicted the tempest that was brewing on the baseball diamond. Even before the first pitch was tossed, there lingered over the game a cloud of unsettling intensity. The mixed races of the Havana-exiled Copacabana Kings looked an unkempt, rough bunch of characters, muttering to each other in ghetto Spanish, playing cards and casting sidelong glances at the local citizenry. Matters fell further afoul when the teams took to the field, as the Seep Selects nine were jeered at, stared at and spat upon by ill-mannered Cubanos.

Finally, in the top of the fifth inning, with our boys leading 3-2, the cauldron boiled over. An errant slider tossed by Farmboy Cody (who is, as is well known in these parts, and by the professional baseball recruiters, a smoke-throwing left-hander, but wild) struck their hulking first baseman, Luis Sugarcane Santiago, in the neck. Pandemonium reigned as the Hispanics stormed the mound. Like their communistic brethren who sacked Havana on New Year's Day, they set upon the Seep players with fiendish fury. The intensity of the Cuban attack at first overwhelmed our boys, unaccustomed as they are to the vicious temper that lurks ever near the surface of the Latinos and Negroes who filled the roster of the visiting side. Hooray for those brave citizens who entered the fray to defend on the Selects' behalf...

Uncle Alex's account dominated the front page, continued on page two for a full ten column inches. His take: the Cubans were mad-dog aggressors, the Seep Selects pacific victims. He made no mention of the spiking by Sugarcane, or the blindside poleaxing of the Cuban manager by Stitch Washington.

And in the very last paragraph of Uncle Alex's story:

> Amidst the brouhaha of the brawl, another voice was heard, the cry of a newborn. During the riot, Mrs. Lance (Ellie) Eliot, wife of the intrepid Dr. Lance Eliot who was so busy with the riot and aftermath, delivered a new addition to the community. Dwight John Eliot was born at the game. Congratulations to Dr. and Mrs. Eliot.

This was the way the story was told by some of those who remembered it — Dwight's father died when he was ten, a full twenty-five years before he got the bee in his bonnet to gather the remnants of the story; by then Uncle Alex drooled his days away in an extended care hospital in Regina. From the time he was a young man Dwight cajoled the story out of the town; as he entered his late thirties he went after it in earnest, making it the subject of his graduate school thesis. For four years, until the age of forty, Dwight spent many afternoons urging old-timers to recount the tale of the Cuban Baseball Riot, as most around Sheepshorn Municipal District referred to it.

Dwight became an accepted curiosity piece, driving all the way from Calgary or wherever he was in his dented and rusty maroon '78 vw van or Jeep truck or Mazda GLC. Dwight witnessed the towns of New and Old Seep dissolving — not dying, because dying would mean it was a living thing. The hotel in Old Seep burned down during his first visit back, was rebuilt, then burned down again for good before his last. The Petro-Canada service station closed (before Petro-Canada, it was Gulf, before that BA, before that, White Rose) — the digging up of the underground storage tanks and clean up of the polluted soil good for a few weeks' work for some local contractors and labourers. The Wheat Pool ceased operations of the only elevator when he was a boy, and it was sold to a seed cleaning operation, which went bankrupt by the time he was making his archive. They eased it onto its side like a sick giraffe, and hauled it all the way to Didsbury, three days at three kilometres per hour. Jim Peebles, long-resigned from the RCMP, and his father-in-law Henry Potsma wrangled a Western Regional Diversification grant to establish a fish farm in the old curling rink in the company side of town. Never produced a trout, but they wintered in Phoenix. The six-bed hospital on the company side of the river was moth-balled decades ago, a victim of cutbacks and apathy. A doctor hadn't lived in town since Dwight's father died in 1969. The UFA store, the five-and-dime, Prince Hal's Fine Clothes, all closed. A few businesses hung on, doing desultory trade, waiting for Godot.

The hydro dam at the falls hummed smartly along with little human interference. IHC (Dwight's ex-employer, who morphed over the years from Prairie Mountain Light & Power into an international energy giant, leveraging its Alberta base and its deep integration into the local and political landscape over a hundred years, from hydro to coal to oil to gas to everything everywhere) slowly closed its side of the town year by year, shifted the operations centre to Calgary. Maintenance workers commuted from the city as necessary.

When Dwight first used to come to Seep to collect his story, he stopped at Alfie Ma's Brown-Eyed Susan Cafe in Old Seep for a plate of vegetarian chow mein. He would fill in Alfie and Rose on his mother's latest medical condition, promise to wish her well from them. Rose always served him a piece of apple pie — on the house, just like your dad. Dwight always ate it, though he didn't particularly fancy apple pie. He visited his old neighbour, his surrogate "mom," Mrs. Holowatzky, at the dry goods store. She bought it out after Goldman died, had saved enough from thirty years' wage as a part-time clerk and babysitter/housekeeper to purchase the business and building outright, despite protests from her husband, who by that time had retired as a lineman for IHC. Mrs. H. rattled off the gossip to Dwight: who died, who moved away, who moved in; how the new people in the old Van Astel house went to Malcolm to buy materials for the drapes, how Miss Flock and Miss Kuntz can't keep up their tick, so she no longer extends credit. She was the second-last resident in New Seep, renting the same house her husband had moved them into in 1938. Her husband died, then she died just before he was in Seep the last time ten years ago. An auctioneer sold off the stock in the dry goods store.

During those years collecting the story, Dwight would eventually wander over the bridge into New Seep to Laugh Jack's barbershop, portable tape recorder slung over his shoulder. News of his presence would precede him. Laugh Jack's was the last business left on that side of the river, and Jack himself the last resident. There were always three or four men from the area waiting. The locals dropped their cagey mistrust of city folk, and forgave him his long hair and earrings, the crude tattoos — ☮ and LVOE — on his forearms. Short sides and top, Laugh Jack deadpanned when Dwight walked in, and the others laughed — Jim Peebles, Henry Potsma, Enos Stelbach, Mike Kowalski, whoever happened along. They all laughed except for Laugh Jack, who never learned to turn up the corners of his mouth, who earned his nickname from the teasing: C'mon, lighten up. Laugh, Jack! And Dwight always replied, Naw, Jack, it's thin enough on top, patting his forehead where the hairline tracked his age, then Dwight swept his hand back to where the hair gathered in a loose ponytail. Dwight would rub his palm over his chin, the skritch of stubble resounding in his head, and say, I think I will take a shave, Jack. Jack would turn away and begin to strop his razor with even thwacking strokes.

In those past trips, Dwight put the tape recorder on a low table with legs fashioned from moose antlers, been in the shop since he was a boy. Enos Stelbach whistled a sucking drag through the plastic tip of his White Owl, blew smoke slowly from his nose, just breathing it out, ignored the chrome airplane ashtray that would fetch a fortune in a collector's shop in the city, preferred to let the cigar ash fall in lumps into the pocket of the brown or blue or green workshirt stretched over his gut. Jim Peebles, nervous Jim Peebles, worked a hangnail, tugged an earlobe, shuffled his feet non-stop, his black brogues (still wearing those cop shoes) scraping splinters off the floorboards exposed through decades-old linoleum. Flies spotted a Seep UFA calendar, decorated with a faded rotogravured farm scene, time stopped in July 1948; the day Jack opened the shop marked with a neat tick of a purple indelible pencil. On hot summer days, the air conditioner over the door would rattle the window; on muggy days heavy with humidity, perhaps a thundershower looming, perhaps only a bluff of rain, it spilled condensation from the drip pan under the coil onto the sidewalk out front, so that the concrete developed a shallow depression where the water gathered in a puddle. Everyone knew to step over when entering, because Laugh Jack was fussy and neat, he cottoned to no one who left a footprint on his threshold. Dwight made room for the tape recorder among the squared stacks of hunting magazines and out-of-date sportfishing regulations and issues of *National Geographic*, and he asked the assembled, Mind if I turn this on?

Mike Kowalski reached deep in his diaphragm, hawked and spit a stream of tobacco juice into a paper cup. Haven't you heard that goddamned baseball story just about enough, someone would say. But no one objected when Dwight pressed RECORD. Then he climbed into the one good chair Jack had left (the other only a cast iron skeleton), the red leather crackled under the weight, the horsehair stuffing packed cheek-shape. Jack working a floor pedal, gliding the lever on the side chair. Head dipping, feet rising, until Dwight was supine. Laugh Jack fished into the towel samovar with a pair of pewter tongs to select the right hot towel in which to swathe Dwight's face.

At first, the small talk between the men ignored Dwight — the weather, crops, so-and-so's new Chevy Silverado, how much such-and-such gambled away in the bars in Caxton or Malcolm on the video lottery machines. Jack lifted the first towel from Dwight's face, then worked a minty, musky cleanser over cheek and jowl. Another hot towel. A voice wondered whether the casino on "Indian" land would ever be built and whether it would make the video lottery and gambling addiction worse. One or two who had heard the rumours of Dwight's personal history with gambling might have cast a sidelong glance to see if there was any reaction under the swaddle of towels. Questions launched at Dwight: You still going to university. The second towel unwound. When the hell you ever going to work with all that education. Another elixir applied to the face: oil. A neutral, mineral smell. Who the hell would hire you. Laugh Jack's hand a caress. The third towel.

Dwight answered, voice muffled by terrycloth, I'm getting educated, you know that. A voice filtering through the heat: A librarian, he's going to be a librarian. What town needs a library. What a crock. Guffaws all around.

And hidden beneath the steaming blank mask, Dwight smiled, but didn't say: I agree, what a crock. Every occupation judged on whether the town needs it. This town with dwindling needs. An aging student in graduate school because he couldn't hold a job. Stretched his education over years — this wasn't something these men wanted to think about.

The third towel now pulled away. With his badger-hair brush, Laugh Jack daubed the hot shaving soap from a mug onto Dwight's face. They ask about his brother, how's the mother.

Now the razor. Another voice: Shame about your old man, he was a good doctor. The only doctor many of them had known personally. Jack's hand steady as a dog on point. Deft strokes of the blade. Jack used his free hand to pull at the flesh, stretching planes of face for the run of razor. The sharp edge nearly soundless, just a whisper of work. No one speaks for a few minutes as they bear witness to the ministration of the shave. Jack's thin face just inches from Dwight's. Blue eyes magnified as if by a jeweller's loupe through the lenses of his wireframe glasses. Gravity tugs at Jack's slack and seamed skin, gathering in comfortable sacks at the cheeks and sags along the jaw.

The first pass finished, another towel. The men resume the banter: Dwight, you get married again, yet? someone wondered and they dropped hints that he must be gay. Let them think what they will, too complicated to explain Sara, with whom he shared his life at that time ten or fourteen years ago. Or his first wife, Sandi-now-Esther. Or his second, Catherine. Lost custody of his own children, one to each. He didn't want the men to touch him there. Under the hot towel, nothing could touch him.

The fourth towel lifted, more hot lather. The second pass of the steel, this time against the grain of his beard. The detail work under the nose, at the sideburns. The last hot towel. You started kicking and screaming to get out about the time the field managers were giving the lineup cards to Hinky Stroh, the umpire, god rest his sanctified-Baptist bastard soul, someone said. The fifth and last hot towel removed, the soft lotion applied — Laugh Jack scorned alcohol-base aftershaves — then the shock of the ice-cold wrap for a half minute to close the pores. Around the table, the story unfolded, ever the same, ever with variations. A cloudless sky, pending hailstorms, calm, a wind blowing hard to right-centre.

That's how Dwight usually told the story, over beers in a tavern (he nursed a soda with lime), after work, maybe catching the World Series on a big-screen TV — the story of The Day I Was Born And A Riot

44

Broke Out With A Visiting Cuban Baseball Team. Dwight waxed nostalgic, he embellished, just as he heard the men do in Laugh Jack's barbershop. His mother's onset of labour timed to the *basso profundo* of Hinky Stroh's "Play ball." The beanball described as the sound of a roast of beef dropped on a tile floor. He invented the detail of an impression of a baseball etched in Sugarcane Santiago's neck, such that he could read the Rawlings trademark in the mirror as he shaved. He likened the splinter of Ed Zosky's leg snapping with the high spiking by Sugarcane on the very next pitch to the shatter of a broken-bat single. When he told the story in a tavern, Dwight synchronized his arrival into the world to match his father negotiating the release of Beulah Howse and the 23 skidoo exit of the Cubans. He succumbed to the temptation to relate the events of the day as he thought his listeners wanted to hear them, as anecdote, perhaps gently — ever so gently — questioning the complacency of a small Alberta town comfortable in its cold war intolerance.

Dwight told the story of a baseball riot that erupted over a beanball, a spiking, the motley Cubans thrown in as an exotic angle, all the variations and inconsistencies at once, how the Cubans took on the entire population of the farmers of Sheepshorn MD and the millwrights of International Heat & Coal, fighting a running battle across the diamond. They swung Louisville Sluggers like pickaxe handles, crashed through the left-field fence, launched roundhouse punches and groin kicks, rolled over the railway tracks, through a fallow field to where someone — who exactly? the Cubans? Stitch Washington? — holed up in Beulah Howse's shack at the edge of town. He described how his mother broke her water, went into contractions, how Dwight was born during this madcap riotous adventure. And in this rendering he played the characters for laughs, registered a tone of apology for the ignorance of the times, a cluck-clucking of the tongue that stumbled over that which should call the game fixed, the father alcoholic, the town racist.

What Dwight didn't tell, nor did any of the old-timers in the barbershop, almost all of whom disappeared over the years, dead, retired to the Sunshine Coast, moved into main-floor bedrooms of sons or daughters in the city of Calgary, until even the barbershop disappeared, shuttered, and only Laugh Jack remained in his weathered, company-owned, shiplap-sided bungalow, nor any others whose interviews are mouldering in boxes of disintegrating mini-cassettes, in reams of transcribed notes, on stacks of 5x7 index cards, all neatly cross-referenced in his filing boxes over the years of research, what none of them who have been telling this story over and over since 1959 acknowledged was this: whatever happened, happened because of ignorance, because of greed, hate, xenophobia, racism. Because the story they didn't tell was the story of all this and more, because the people who told this story still lived this and more until they were gone and only the stories remained. And if they did know, they forgot it all in a bottle, or at the hollow end of a shotgun. For if they did remember, it was at their peril.

If this story touched on baseball, it reached out from the community, from a town where the school principal and Scout Master bullied his sons, the editor of the town paper beat his wife, the town druggist injected morphine he short-prescribed to the hospital, the town doctor drank still whisky, the Lutheran pastor's wife slept with men not her husband because her husband slept with a revolver, the Mountain Meadow Queen was pregnant, the town constable the father, the dogs were all rabid, the cats distemperate.

No. They — and Dwight — who used to tell this story, told it much like Uncle Alex did in his newspaper, Uncle Alex who is nobody's uncle, who took delight in pinching children's arms black-and-blue (ridiculing those who dared cry out), who broke his wife's cheekbone with a closed fist in a drunken rage, who masturbated under his desk watching schoolgirls pass by his office window — Uncle Alex, whose only redeeming quality was that he fathered no children of his own. This is how Dwight had intended to tell the story as part of his thesis, a col-

46

lected oral history, replete with inaccuracy and the voices of recondite liars — shadowy nostalgia with queer contradictions, brimming with laughable lummoxes and shot through with colourful detail. His brother Darcy remembered only that Luis Santiago wore red shoes. His father set Ed Zosky's leg with pieces of the outfield fence. His mother went into labour under the grandstand. His father refused to help her because he loved baseball, and a good thing because they needed his level head and someone to stitch the wounded, too.

The story Dwight wanted to tell was one of a W. O. Mitchell aw-shucks toe-in-the-dirt prairie-meets-mountain town, peopled with kids named Duke or Wally who spent summers flying kites on the wind their teacher sees all the way to the vanishing point of the flat horizon. A Kinsella-esque baseball story starring a charismatic red-shod Cuban fleeing Fidel, a legendary wild pitcher named Farmboy whose fastball traced the air with smoke. A story complete with thrilling grass, dreamy fields and conspiracies of memory that defied a single inter-pretation. He intended to relate how he had reconstructed the myriad details of the day he was born, complete with riddles that he had been unable to solve despite years of tortuous research. He intended to let the reader discover for herself the dark threads embedded in the weave of the tale in the same way Dwight had discovered them — by a clever deciphering of clues uncovered by forensic librarianship: a partially completed scorecard, newspaper clippings, interviews with aging men in a barbershop. In the Preface he never wrote for the thesis that he never completed, he would have said:

        I am compelled to intervene in my own text;
        I cannot be coy about the misery that festers in
        the heart of my history. If I choose to tell
        this story conventionally, to eke out informa-
        tion in veiled allusion, in crafted sub-text, if
        I dole out the episodes selectively to punch up

47

the ending, to draw tears and laughter at whim, if I harbour certain secrets only to loose them for dramatic effect, if I construct an arbitrary dynamic narrative of exposition-climax-denouement, would that not be as great a conceit as I indulge in now? Let me state what I know: many of the people in this story, in my life, were immoral, hypocritical. They were malevolent, confused. They acted from fear, from malice. They were bigots or worse. They lied, they cheated, they stole. Some were held in esteem by their community, they wielded authority like a cudgel, and woe betide those who challenged. They were fathers, mothers, children. They are where I am from. This is a story punctured by a wintry summer evening in Laugh Jack's living room, listening to him fold back the cover of the town like a mildewed blanket. Of yearning to hold my mother as she scribbles awkward truths on scraps of paper that have replaced her cancerous larynx, her sobs silent, the notes never passed to my hand.

That was after the last time he came to Seep, ten years ago.

When I met your father I had no idea that the best of his career was already behind him. He was truly Errol Flynn — or maybe more like Montgomery Clift. Handsome. Dark. Brooding. The war was five years past. I was just twenty, returned home to Squamish with a newly minted nursing diploma. They had built a new hospital in Ocean Falls in Cousins Inlet, so off I went with a huge cardboard suitcase on the three ferry rides to get there from the remote pulp and paper town I grew up in to another even more remote pulp and paper town. They used to build hospitals in small towns in those days. They used to build whole towns. And here was Lance, smart, Columbia-trained, American war-hero doctor, just turned thirty-two, full of energy and hope and Yankee enthusiasm. Nobody thought to ask: "Why here? Why Ocean Falls?" We all thought we were in paradise. A mill town with no road access where it rained three hundred days a year. Paradise.

4.

The Stars Reveal Themselves

11 May 2009

Dwight stopped at the new casino on his way to the city after seeing Amy among the earthmovers. Here the fruits of colonial exploitation and decolonial opposition found synthesis in the capitalization of gaming. The casino was finally open after fifteen years of finagling, but the hotel was still under construction. The sign said, Yes! We have rooms! The half of the building that contained the rooms was encased in scaffold. Gusts snapped at the tarpaulins that shrouded the worksite. The new black asphalt beamed in the late morning light, with bright yellow lines marking empty space. Plantless planters and trapezoid shaped medians devoid of landscaping marked the boundaries of the parking lot. Last year's tumbleweeds drifted by.

Dwight was trying not to be all the men he had ever been or ever would be, who had been in all the casinos, games rooms, VLT lounges, racetracks, dog tracks that he had ever been to. He tried to forget Las Vegas junkets, the lost weekend in Atlantic City, the twelve hours once spent at the Calgary Stampede, The Greatest Outdoor Show on Earth, where he never left the booth with the Over/Under wheel except to purchase and pass corn dogs and iced cold root beer and sugared mini-donuts. He tried not to be the man who had once lost a half year's salary on a boxing match. That one ended his second marriage.

When Dwight finally got out of the car he locked his wallet with his bank card in the trunk of his Toyota. He had two ten-dollar bills in his shirt pocket. Ten dollars on nickel slots, he told himself. Ten dollars more just in case.

The wind blew hard here, across an open flat. A golf swing away, the traffic sped past on the highway. The plan was to build a road across the reserve land to connect the newly imagined development at Seep with the casino and highway. Before he got out of the car, but after he had decided to go in, he felt the dread calm settle over him. The dread of the loss. The dread of the win. That old friend. Action. His breathing eased and slowed. His hand was steady and did not shake. No moisture on his palms. His mouth was very dry, as if the wind had somehow permeated his head to scour his tongue and extract all saliva. He had become all the men he ever was and would be. He hadn't placed a bet in fourteen years. It's like riding a bicycle, he thought. One of those old English bicycles like the angels ride on a deck of Bicycle cards.

On his second trip back to the car in the parking lot, he brought the wallet in with him. When he left, finally, darkness had fallen and the moon shone. He had spent all the cash in his wallet, and withdrawn his daily limit on his bank debit card. He had resisted the urge to take cash advances from his credit card. At one point, he had been ahead nearly $3,000 at the roulette table. But when they finally opened the craps game, a run of cold dice drew him down. He leaned against his car. The wind blew through openings in the half-built hotel, sounding a low breathy note like a bassoon. He watched the stars reveal themselves. That really bright one is Venus, he thought. He would bet on it.

Of course he swept me off my feet. He bought a beautiful boat, not a working boat or an open fishing boat, but a sleek cabin cruiser with an inboard motor and a mahogany deck. We would dash up and down the sound, have picnics in isolated inlets. Rain or shine, usually rain. He talked about getting a pilot's licence and his own plane so we could fly to Vancouver for dinner. We were married within the year, had Darcy in two, and by the third year were searching for a "new situation." I didn't find out until Darcy was born that he had been married before. I don't imagine you knew that either until you read it just now. He swore to me he was divorced from the first, but I never saw any papers. He swore to me there were no children. I believed that. He tried to talk me out of having Darcy. By the time I was pregnant with you we didn't really talk.

5.

Hello! My Name Is

19 May 2009

Dwight began to go to meetings about Seep. A week after seeing his home at the head of the Waldron, he drove to the public open house at the Birdwing Community Hall, hosted by the developer. Birdwing was another whistle stop, east of the town, between Seep and Caxton. He timed it so that he could visit the casino before and after the meeting.

The hall was north from the river, down a range road. A small sign pointed the way from the highway: Birdwing Community Hall 8 KM. Dwight missed the next turn. He was massaging the wad of $100 bills in his pocket. High-stakes blackjack table. The casino had been almost empty, and for most of the afternoon he had the only seat at the table. Un-interrupted action, one hand after another. His stack of chips grew, until it was time to go before he had begun to lose. It was dark now, no moon. There was no light at the turnoff, and he drove until his odometer told him he had gone eleven kilometres. He had forty-six bills in the wad.

He double-backed to the turn, and snaked along a road that traced the curves of a nameless creek. The hall was a Quonset with a gabled porch appended to its centre to mark the entrance. A dozen vehicles were parked on the gravel apron — SUVs, muddied ranchers' 4x4's, two panel vans with SmarTec Consulting logos on their sides: Planning Solutions. His was the only sedan.

He pulled to the edge of the lot, just outside the pool of orange thrown by the sodium glow of the yard light. He got out and stood in the night. For a moment, he turned his back on the building. The low humps of foothills were black against the starry sky. The stars. He looked at the night sky without marvel, aware he was without marvel. Once, he could name a score of stars, pick out the major constellations of Cassiopeia and Orion, and a few minor ones too, like Draco and Cepheus. He knew the transits of the planets. Now he was vaguely aware the Big Dipper was somewhere over his right shoulder, along with Polaris, but he didn't turn to seek them out. He wasn't even sure what phase the moon was in, only that it hadn't risen yet, or had already set.

He approached the hall; the door swung open when he was half a dozen steps away. A rectangular hole of incandescent light opened into the darkness. A woman filled the door frame. She looked like somebody's mother, though not quite old enough to be his own mother. The thought "costume" floated in his head as he took her in — she was dressed like she belonged at the door to a farmhouse or in a ranch kitchen, but in a ranch kitchen displayed in a magazine spread about ranch kitchens. Her pressed jeans were tucked in weathered cowboy boots. The pearled-button checked shirt was open at the collar, and her neck covered by a paisley kerchief knotted cowboy-style. C'mon in! she hailed.

Dwight stepped to one side to let her pass. After you, he said.

She hesitated. Her smile never faltered but for a second. She coolly assessed his lumpy cross-trainers, his baggy blue jeans, his untucked sport shirt, his rumpled windbreaker. He stuck his hand in his pocket and clenched the roll of hundreds. Then the register of awareness as she put the moment in its place.

Oh no, I'm not going out. I opened the door to let you in. Get in here out of the cold. She beckoned, and he entered.

Inside the door, two folding tables draped with checked tablecloths. The smell of percolating coffee and fresh baking. One table held an urn, a harlequin set of enamelled coffee cups, lumps of cane sugar in a cut-glass bowl, and cream in an earthenware jug. A plate of chocolate chip cookies and another of tarts. I'm glad you could make it, she said, as if he were an old friend and expected guest. An adhesive name tag affixed over her left breast: Hello! My Name Is Miriam.

We're asking folks to sign in, the woman said. And we have a draw for a night at the Banff Springs Hotel if you'd like to drop your business card in here. She pointed to a gallon-sized pickling jar.

Dwight thought of the obsolete cards he had in his wallet, with his old work number. I didn't bring any cards, he said.

Well. Let's get you a name tag. Miriam smiled sweetly. She had a Sharpie uncapped and poised to write.

Dwight looked at the cordon of tables at the entrance where Miriam presided. A surprising number of people milled about, more than were suggested by the collection of vehicles outside. Display tables were set along one wall, with foam-core boards showing graphic representations of street layouts and land use zones and elevations of townhomes. At one end of the hall, a flat-screen monitor played a loop of video to twenty folding chairs. Knots of people stood by the tables, where consultants and management types explained the finer points of the New Seep redevelopment.

Your name, Miriam said, not exactly a question.

Dwight looked at her, and at the pen. Jon, he said.

She wrote: J-O-H-N.

No H, Dwight said. Just Jon, J-O-N.

Okey-dokey, Jon. Miriam made a new tag and with efficient dexterity peeled it from its backing and placed it smartly on Dwight's shirt, gently pulling aside the lapel of his jacket. He could smell the Purell on her hands. We're informal here tonight, Miriam said. Just a chance to see the work we're doing, and to ask questions. What was your last name? Miriam had turned again to the table, and a guest book there. She had conjured a ballpoint pen.

Andersson, Dwight said. Jon Andersson. Two S's. In Andersson.

Okey-dokey. No H Jon, two S Andersson. Phone number, she asked? Dwight rattled off his home number. He hadn't used that number for years, used only his cellphone now.

A man detached himself from a group in the hall and approached Dwight. He was Dwight's age, fit, square-jawed. His faded Wranglers broke over lace-up roper boots. His shirt was a another pearled-button job, but a solid unpatterned burgundy. He wore a loose faded buckskin jacket with intricate beadwork and rawhide-sewed seams. Simon! Miriam said. I was just letting Jon here know what we were doing tonight.

Before he even realized he was doing it, Dwight automatically reached his hand out to meet the other man's. Simon seized Dwight's hand confidently. Dwight concentrated on returning the grip, not wanting to give the cold-fish shake.

Jon, the man said. Pleased to meet you, Jon. I'm Simon Love. His name tag wasn't handwritten, but engraved on a badge and held fast to his jacket with a pin: S. Love, Chairman.

Dwight couldn't stop himself from saying: It's a shame to put a pin through that buckskin.

What's that? Simon said.

Your name tag. Pinned to your jacket. Puncturing the leather. Dwight's first wife had studied textiles in art school, before she found Jesus. This jacket belonged in a museum.

This old thing? Simon looked down and patted the jacket front. Oh it's seen worse. Simon steered Dwight to a display in the hall. It was a gift from my partner, Tom Peacock. Isn't that right, Tom? The man Simon addressed looked up from where he was studying a miniature model of the new New Seep. This man had long greying braids that framed his face. He was about Dwight's age, and Dwight thought he was vaguely familiar. Most of the reserve kids lived downstream, closer to Caxton, and went to their own school in the village of Arundel, so

Dwight had had little contact with them when he was growing up. Another manifestation of the xenophobia, he supposed. I was telling Jon here how this jacket was a gift from you.

Tom looked at the jacket, then at Dwight. Wasn't my idea, Tom said. It was my grandfather's jacket. He shrugged. He looked down again at the model which was spread under a dome-shaped plastic cover, like a dessert at a fancy restaurant. Replicas of stone-clad condos and larger close-set single family homes, also stone-clad were laid out like petits fours along clean streets with marshmallow sidewalks. Perfect trees like mint lollipops. The dam looked like a layer cake set in the blue frothy icing of the river. Miniature cars like marzipan wedges, caught in unmoving time on the roads; tiny pedestrians like the sugar-candy brides and grooms on a wedding cake, except these ones were detailed to look as if they had just stepped off the golf course. There was even a wee brown dog: chocolate Lab. Behind the diorama, a bifold panel showed representations of the proposed town plan, colour-coded for land use. Industrial, commercial, areas for residential. There was a typo, Dwight noticed.

Wings on either side of the plan displayed collages of photos — historical photos of the falls from before the dams, a portrait of Chief Reginald Peacock that Dwight recognized, landscapes, the mountains at sunset. A coyote on a ridge. A group of men curling on an outdoor rink. Was that his father, holding a flask?

Simon talked, gesturing to the plan, to the model. Re-imagining. Development investment. Opportunity. Potential. Need. Density. Dwight interrupted: You spelled residential wrong.

What? Simon said.

Your poster. It's missing the i in residential. It says "residental."

Simon paused; he looked at the display, then turned square to Dwight, staying just far enough away to not be encroaching on the limits of personal space. You're right, he said. You've got an eye for detail. I admire that in a person. We'll fix that.

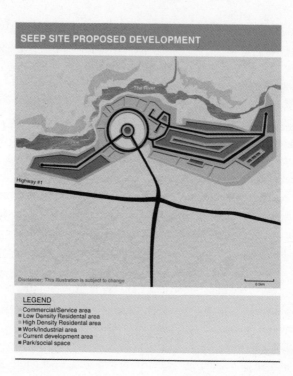

SEEP SITE PROPOSED DEVELOPMENT

The River

Highway #1

Disclaimer: This illustration is subject to change

0.5km

LEGEND
Commercial/Service area
■ Low Density Residental area
▓ High Density Residental area
■ Work/Industrial area
▒ Current development area
■ Park/social space

Tom stood up and put his hands in the back pockets of his jeans. He wandered away while Simon continued talking. Beauty. Recreation. Management. Responsibility.

Dwight sensed someone was next to him. Jesus, Amy. Don't sneak up on me like that, Dwight said.

Simon said: Oh, you two know each other. Another sizing-up gaze.

Oh yeah, Amy said. Jon — she stretched the name out — and I go back a long ways. Did he tell you he was born in Seep?

Is that so, Simon said.

Yes, Dwight said. He pointed through the dome over the model of the future to a circular plaza with an ersatz baroque fountain. Right about here.

Amy was in her security uniform. She looked to the door. Talk to you later, Jon, she said. Simon looked at Amy and raised an eyebrow.

Any sign of unusual guests, Simon said. Dwight thought he detected a hint of a glance directed his way.

Everything is cool, Amy said. No worries.

Simon steered Dwight — gently, mind — to two men who were standing by another display. The Water of Life, a banner proclaimed. Bill, why don't you show Jon here the water treatment plan.

Hiya Jon, Bill said. He was a bear of a man, with a gut that lolled beneath a lumberjack shirt untidily tucked into cargo pants. His nametag was a custom job too. SmarTec Environmental. Bill. He started talking. Underground aquifer. Ten kilometres of stainless pipe. Water for the whole valley, and not a drop from the river watershed. In fact, Bill said, we're adding to the river flow. Lookee here, he said, and pointed to the map.

Tom was standing beside him again, sipping a coffee. Did he say, "lookee here"? Dwight asked him. Tom shrugged.

The discharge from the wastewater plant is above the dam, Bill said. So we're adding to the flow through the power plant.

Isn't that upstream of the town? Dwight asked.

That's right, Bill said.

But won't you have to pump the water above the falls? I mean won't that take more energy?

Oh no, not really, Bill said. It's an offset situation. You see, Jon, the power we generate with the flow offsets the power we need for the lift stations.

Wouldn't it be easier just to let gravity do the work? Dwight asked.

You're a man with a lot of questions, Jon, Bill said. I like that. Gravity may *seem* like the best solution. His enthusiasm never wavered.

It's a plan, now, Bill said. We can always change it.

Then he heard his name. Dwight! He turned. A young woman was coming to him. Willow: Amy's daughter. Uncle Dwight, she said, laughing with surprise. She turned to some people who were with her. Clearly, these were the unusual guests — young men with matted dreadlocks, granola moms with babies in slings, two grannies that must be raging. It's my uncle, Willow said, and she ran to him and hugged him.

Simon Love and Hello! My Name Is Miriam had edged over to where they could confer with Amy. Another beefy man in a jean jacket that stretched at the seams across his shoulders joined them. More security, but plainclothes. The beefy man looked into Dwight's eyes.

Dwight felt the money in his pocket, and imagined dice bouncing on green felt.

There is no easy way to write this. Your father performed abortions. That in itself is not necessarily earth-shattering news. And in this day and age we can understand that for a medical doctor to do such a thing can be a compassionate act. He used that logic on me. If he didn't do it, using his medical training, knowledge and skill, there was the risk of some back-alley butcher doing it. In those days it was always a back-alley butcher. As you can imagine, in a small isolated community, with no roads in, it is hard to keep such a thing secret. In theory, I didn't object to the abortions. We hadn't gone through the whole women's lib movement yet, but I was an educated woman. I had seen enough girls get married to bullet-headed loggers because they were in the family way, and go to live in a hovel in the woods and raise baby after baby. I had known the girls who suddenly went to live with an aunt in Regina for a few months, only to return to high school sadder and wiser and lonelier.

6.

I Always Find You

3 June 2009

Dwight Eliot came home one night — more like morning, 4:37 by his Toyota's digital clock. Eight minutes fast. In his car he was always just that much of the man he imagined he was in the future. He had spent hours at the new casino in the city — not the one on the reserve, not that reserve, but the newer one, on the reserve that butts up to the Calgary city limits. He had $6,326 in his pocket. Tonight he was a winner. With tonight's take, he estimated he was nearly $11,000 in the hole since he stopped at the casino near Seep a few weeks ago. He parked in front of his house. Lights burned in every window. The front door was open, though the screen door was shut. The sounds of an electric guitar boomed from inside. Not complete songs, but phrases — a few chords of Jimi's "Purple Haze." Then into "Sweet Home Alabama." Some Black Sabbath riffs morphing into free-form shredding.

He had known this moment was coming. It always came, sooner or later. He had known ever since his mother passed him that note on Mother's Day — "Darcy called." Dwight sat in his car. The late night CBC broadcast was airing a bit from Radio Netherlands English Service — controversy about a wind farm next to a Great War cemetery in Belgium. He listened until the clock beamed 4:44.

His brother stepped through the door and stood on the concrete block of a porch, shirtless, barefoot. The Fender Telecaster strapped across his hard fat belly. Despite the gut's ample size, Dwight knew it was firm enough to bounce quarters off of. Darcy still noodled the strings. Iron Butterfly now, innagaddadavida, baby. Darcy turned and wandered back inside, showing the greasy ass of his jeans to the bird-chirping morning of the world.

Dwight entered the house and stood in the small space that served as the front hall to his cookie-cutter 1950s bungalow. Darcy occupied the centre of the living room, now windmilling through a medley of Pete Townshend chord progressions — "My Generation" and "Won't Get Fooled Again" and all that, then deftly transitioning to Neil Young, "Rust Never Sleeps." Dwight kept a simple house, not fanatically clean, not freaky, but tidy. In the few hours he had been away, since Darcy found his way in, things had changed.

A woman was asleep on the couch, on her back, mouth agape, one eye half open. The half-open eye was eerie, but Dwight knew she was alive because she was snoring. She wore a satiny cowboy shirt, the pearl buttons snapped all the way up to her neck. She wasn't wearing any pants, just a cheap pair of men's tighty-whities. Beer cans littered surfaces everywhere, on their sides, upside down, on the coffee table, on the floor, on the mantel of the gas fireplace. A nearly empty forty-pounder of Jack Daniel's was on the bench seat built into the bay window. Two half-eaten pizzas spilled out of their boxes on chairs brought over from the dining nook. Cigarette butts crammed a coffee cup. One of the beer cans had been flattened and fashioned into a pipe. Dwight could smell the beer, and cigarettes, and marijuana. He wasn't sure if he could detect a higher, chemical smell too. Darcy chopped out a shave and a haircut two bits, and then stopped playing. He opened his arms as if to say, Ta-da! The two brothers looked at each other.

Hello Darcy, Dwight said. This is a non-smoking house.

Man, you need a *dog*, Darcy said. A place like this *needs* a dog.

Long time no see, Dwight said.

I love this guitar, man. It's a fucking masterpiece. 1964 Fender Tellie. You stole this guitar from me. I mean stole it. Like, what did you give me for this? Two hundred bucks? You stole it, man.

Make yourself at home. Dwight remained at the threshold to his own house.

Do you have any gas? We ran out of gas. Darcy plucked out the first notes of "Jumpin' Jack Flash." It's a gas gas gas, he said. I still got my chops, man. You hear that? I can play this motherfucker. I *never* should have sold this to you. Never. It's worth thousands, now. Darcy made a gesture with his hand that held the guitar pick. We ran out of gas. He waved toward the window, the street, the city. Somewhere out there. Close. We're close. We got real close. Shelley and me. Sherry. Here. Shelley. Darcy prodded the sleeping woman's dirty bare foot. She didn't stir. We were driving *here*, man. You got a jerry can?

You ran out of gas. Dwight moved a couple of steps into the living room. There was nowhere to sit. The woman was on the couch. A knapsack was on one of the chairs. A handbag fashioned from braided seat belts and a pile of clothes — Darcy's shirt, the woman's pants, jackets, a leather vest — were on the other one. But you managed to acquire cases of beer and Jack Daniel's and pizza, Dwight said.

Dwight, bro. Little brother! Darcy slipped the guitar from his body, propped it in a corner. He turned and opened his arms. His eyes blazed with alcohol and drugs. The sparse hair on his chest and belly was salt and pepper grey. He had tattoos — old-school tattoos, the black fading to blue, the colours that may have once been there washed out to patches of brown and red and green like a collection of old pennies. A parrot on a pectoral. A crude skull on a shoulder. A snake around a forearm. He put his arms down. Dwight was not going to hug him. Darcy smiled and showed his brown and broken teeth. You're always so fucking serious, you little shit, he said.

Who's your friend, Dwight said.

She's got a car. Darcy rocked on his feet, not reeling like a drunk, but rocking like a hyperactive kid. We were partying, and I found out she had a car and I go, let's visit my brother and she goes, where does he live and I go, Calgary, man, he lives in Calgary. And she goes, let's do it. We came to see you.

Really, Dwight said. Where were you, across town?

Oh yeah, we were across town. We were across the universe. Darcy's hands moved as if he was still playing, air-guitaring the Beatles. We were at The Transcona.

Winnipeg, Dwight said.

No, no, not Winnipeg, Darcy said. White Rock, I think. Whatever. Don't be so fucking serious. We got in the car and came here, man. We drove for days, across deserts and mountains. Darcy's hands mimicked the flatness of a desert, and the rise and fall of mountains. We were explorers.

How did you get my address, Dwight said.

Questions, questions, questions. Always with the fucking questions. Darcy wasn't smiling anymore. I found you. I always find you.

Your father did abortions for his girlfriends. In a small town like Ocean Falls there are few secrets. The secrets may take time to come out. And they aren't printed in the paper, or even spoken of in any way that is obvious. But they do emerge. Always. Darcy was six months old when the rumours finally came to me. When I was pregnant with Darcy, Lance had impregnated an eighteen-year-old girl named Betty. Betty was the daughter of a teacher, and one of the members of the small professional social class, and she was going to ubc to study anthropology. Then the rumour about Margaret, the waitress at the Martin Hotel café. If Betty was somewhat younger than Lance, Margaret was somewhat older. But still, apparently, fecund. These were the two I heard about in the roundabout way these things come. Someone contacted someone in Cleveland, where Lance had come from. I found out about the first wife. And the rumours of abortions that had dogged him there too, abortions performed on girlfriends and maybe friends of the girlfriends or girlfriends of friends.

7.

Shiplap

19 July 1969

He always finds him. Once upon a time, Dwight is ten years old. With a stick in his hand. A half-strip of shiplap prised from the side of the house with a hatchet Darcy left buried in the stump. Go out and play, his mother says. She is in the front room of the house in Seep with Laugh Jack, the barber. They are planning Dwight's father's funeral. They sit in the front room, where a clean square on the bare pine-board floor marks the absence of the rug that has been taken up and — and what? Where is it, Dwight wants to ask. Where is the carpet my father bled to death on? Rolled up, taken away. To the dump? Where the coyotes and reserve strays from across the tracks can nose at it, tear it, suck his father's blood? Dwight sits in the middle of the clean square, but doesn't ask these questions. Go and play, his mother says. He goes outside to the waiting hatchet.

He takes the hatchet from the stump, hefts it. The day is grey. A porridge of clouds is drawn across the sky, trapping the summer heat, obscuring the mountains, flattening the light into a sticky, shadowless blankness. Somewhere up beyond the clouds, beyond atmosphere, across a light-second of space, three men in a spacecraft prepare to orbit the moon. Dwight paces off ten steps from the stump, and with each step grasshoppers bound away with the clack of carapace. He throws the hatchet at the stump, attempting to send it end for end the way Darcy and his friends can do it, a flick of the wrist, a flashing arc, occasionally the satisfying *thock!* of blade fixing into the soft meat of the cottonwood stump. Dwight's throw skews and skids to a stop three feet short and a foot wide of the target. He fetches the hatchet and walks to the back door.

He listens through the screen to the cadence of Laugh Jack's tenor voice — he can't hear the words, only the scissored speech patterns. Then his mother — voice raised. I don't care, she says. It's my decision. Then softer, the words lost.

He waves the hatchet, then strikes it lightly into a seam in the wood cladding just to the right of the door. It holds fast. He wiggles the handle, then torques it down with steady pressure. The crack widens and he torques it some more. With a *snap!* the board splits. From inside the house: Is that you Dwight? Yes, mom, he calls back. He drops the hatchet. I told you to go and play, she calls. Yes, mom, he says. He pulls at the strip of wood. It comes away in his hand. Are you still there, she calls again. No, mom, he says. Now he has a stick. Go and play.

Go and play. He goes. He walks towards the river, lopping the heads off the brown-eyed Susans that grow in the ditches beside the road. Father's dead, he says to himself as he swings at each flower with the stick. Father is dead. His esophagus ruptured. Esophagus, he says out loud. He swallows spit so he can feel his own esophagus. Three days ago he wasn't sure what an esophagus was. Dwight slinks through the hole in the fence around the generating station and scrambles down to the river and stands below the control room building. He watches the water spill over the dam. He follows a rough path downstream until it peters out at the river's edge, then he climbs to where the bare rock slants toward the water, then drops off in a twenty-five-foot cliff. This is where Darcy and the older boys come to jump. The river is deep here, swift but not too swift, gathering its volume in a lazy sweep before it enters the chute and the sluice to the lower dam. He stands on the very rim of the rock, where he has never ventured before. He spits into the river, then pisses into the river, holding his penis in his right hand while he waves his stick back and forth in the stream of his own water. My father is dead, he calls to the river, and he is suddenly very scared and he takes a step back, causing him to stipple his pants and shoes with urine. His funeral shoes. They drove into the city earlier that day and got him a pair of new shoes for his father's funeral. He turns and makes his way back to town, eschewing the path.

He swings his stick like a machete at the bracken of willow and scrub alder. Crows caw. Jays screech. He comes out of the bush onto the service road that leads from the plant to the lower dam. A company truck bumps past. The man in the passenger seat looks over. When he sees Dwight, the smile on his face dissolves into a grim expression, and he touches the peak of his hat as if in salute. From the direction of town, a small dog, alone, moves toward him at a skewed canter, its rear end not quite aligned with its front. It is that girl's dog, Amy's. A Heinz 57, terrier and other things. Hello, dog, Dwight says. My father is dead. The dog bows. Its tail wags. His esophagus ruptured. I don't feel like crying. The dog's tail swishes back and forth, back and forth, and it barks, once. We're going to have a funeral. The dog falls in beside him, snapping at the grasshoppers that rise from his feet. You can't come, Dwight says. Mother says no one can come to the funeral. Just us. Dwight walks. The porridge-sky thick across the roof of the world.

Dwight and the dog arrive at the baseball diamond. The foul lines radiate from home plate, the lime mostly erased between home and first and third bases, smudged from half-a-summer's play. Dwight stands on the pitcher's mound and toes the rubber with his new shoes. I was born here, he says to the dog. Right here. His shoes are scuffed and marked with dirt. Not here on the mound, exactly. Over there. He aims the stick at the concession stand behind the bleacher, and the dog tenses, alert, expecting the stick to be thrown. As he waves the stick, Darcy steps from around the side of the shack, as if summoned by a wand. Darcy raises his hand and points at Dwight. I found you, Darcy yells.

He didn't deny it. We were out on that stupid boat. I loved that boat. We were sitting in the cockpit well in the back of the boat, sitting on cushions I had sewed to keep our bums warm on the beautiful mahogany benches. We had drinks. Gin and tonics. His more gin, mine more tonic. Darcy was fussing, spitting out the nipple of the bottle, squirming in my arms. Give him here, your father said, and he took Darcy. We were anchored in a little bay across the inlet. The stacks from the mill spewed their smoke and steam. There was no wind, not the faintest hint of a breeze. The columns of smoke rose straight up until they caught some weather high in the air and bent toward land. The sky was blue, the water like glass. A rare sunshine day. Darcy calmed down and Lance began to drink. I know about Betty, I said. Lance cooed at Darcy, didn't look up. I know about Margaret, I said. Now he looked at me, and said, Who? It was all very civilized to begin with. Like we were talking about the weather, or whether we'd see Tony Bennett when we next went to Vancouver, or whether to recover the couch. I took a sip of my drink. I know about Cleveland, I said. I know you were married.

8.

Risk Management

3-4 June 2009

Darcy slumped to the floor now, back against the couch, head resting on the woman's lower leg. She had tattoos, too. Chinese characters down both shins, a spider's web on one kneecap, a hummingbird on the other. On each thigh, a poker hand, the dead man's hand. Aces and eights: on the left side, clubs and spades, with a Jack of Diamonds as the kicker; on the right, hearts and diamonds, with the Jack of Spades. A split pot, Dwight thought. For the dead man. From the knees down, her legs were toothpick thin, but there was still some muscle on the thigh. Sometime in the past, she had been an athlete, a skier, a speed skater. Aces and eights.

Darcy dug in the fob pocket of his jeans and extracted a foil packet. He wasn't shaking, but his movements were imprecise, fogged with booze. Dwight was about to say something, about to explode, but then was actually relieved to see Darcy spill a bud of marijuana from the foil.

Not the rock, Darcy said, as if reading his brother's mind. Just a bud. Good old-fashioned weed. He broke off half of what he had, the size of a pencil eraser. He picked up the beer-can pipe and put the bud on the grate he'd made by punching holes on a flattened surface near the bottom of the can. He pulled a lighter from his back pocket. He clicked it alive. It was not a regular cigarette lighter — it ignited like a small torch. A crackhead's or a meth-head's flame.

Dwight stood in his living room. His brother found him. He always found him. He stood in his living room, but he was not only standing in his living room. He was younger. He was older. He is all the brothers he could ever be and ever will be to this brother, who always finds him, will always find him. He is driving a frozen vw van over the Waldron. He is a boy with a stick on a pitcher's mound, talking to a dog while his mother and Laugh Jack argue over his father's funeral. He is a young man curled on a cot in an ATCO trailer crying into his grey pillow, twenty years old, Darcy hammering on the door with boots and fists, come out here you fuck you can't fire me you fuck you useless dipshit. He is sitting in a stolen pickup truck, the last time he saw his brother ten years ago, watching Darcy work a lighter like the one he uses now to ignite the marijuana in the makeshift bong. He always finds him.

Dwight gripped the wad of cash in his pocket through the cloth of his khakis. A lump of freedom. Dread freedom. Darcy exhaled the smoke from his hit, fumbled the bong onto the table, spilling the hot coal onto the surface. He leaned back his head and closed his eyes. Dwight looked at the ash on the table, witnessed it burn a mark into the grain of the wood, but made no move to snuff it out. He walked out of his house, drove to the Deerfoot Inn & Casino, paid cash for a room. He slept till noon, played high-stakes baccarat until his cash was gone, and drove back home. It was exactly fourteen hours since he had pulled up to his house that morning. The front door was closed. The curtains were drawn. The lingering heat of the day bore down as he made his way up the sidewalk. He had missed the sunshine, hunched over a table all day. To the west and north cumulonimbus began to stack the sky, harbingers of hail and thunder. Elsewhere in the city, citizens two-stepped their way through the evening at cowboy bars, practicing for the annual Stampede.

Darcy sat in the middle of the couch. His shabby hair swept back

78

from his forehead, tucked behind his ears. It was wet. He wore one of Dwight's shirts. Too small to go over his gut. Only three of the buttons near the top were done up. The bottles and refuse were gone, the knapsack out of sight somewhere. Coffee brewed in the kitchen. The odour of burnt toast hung in the house.

Where's your friend, Dwight asked.

I told her to fuck off, Darcy said.

Is she coming back, Dwight said.

I said, "I told her to fuck off." Like, fuck off, get outta here.

What about the gas, Dwight said.

Darcy looked at him. Where the fuck were you, he said.

Burnt toast, Dwight said. That's an old trick to get rid of bad smells.

Four banker's boxes were piled on the coffee table. Part of Dwight's archive collected years ago. It had been stored downstairs. Darcy picked up a piece of paper he had been looking at. He read aloud, quoting: "'Transcript of interview with John Rees, aka Laugh Jack. Occupation: barber. Location: Laugh Jack's house, Seep, Alberta. Date: July 5, 1999. DE: " That's you, eh. Me too. DE. "So, Jack, how did you end up in Seep?" Fuck. You're something, man. A regular Edgar Rice Burroughs.

Don't touch my stuff, Dwight said. And you mean Edward Murrow.

I know what I mean. "Don't touch my stuff." This crap is pathetic. Nobody gives a rat's ass about you or a bunch of crazy Cubans. The Day You Were Born. Fuck. Darcy rummaged through some of the papers he had spread out, picked out a document in a protective plastic sleeve. You've got the official scorecard for Chrissakes. Dwight moved to take it. Darcy held it up and away. Careful, bro. It might get crumpled. Dwight had the coffee table between him and his brother, and he hesitated, not wanting to knock the boxes on the floor.

Dwight backed off. Get out, he said. Leave.

Darcy tossed the scorecard into the pile of papers. Is that like your birth certificate or something, he said. I got no place to go.

Dwight picked up the baseball scorecard from the table, found its spot in the banker's box. He began sorting the other papers Darcy had disturbed, restoring his archive to order. Don't touch my stuff, he said. You can't stay here.

I got no place to go, Darcy said. I'm clean. I won't be jonesing.

That last time, ten years ago, Darcy detoxing and going through withdrawal in the Smithson's guest house. Sara and Julee arriving at the airport terminal, Darcy in full-blown paranoia and craving. You're clean, Dwight said. All that pot last night, beer, the whisky. The drive over desert and mountain. Dwight waved his hand in imitation of Darcy's rant last night.

Darcy shrugged. A relapse. Just a few days. It's over. Mom says hi.

What? Dwight said.

Mom says hi, Darcy said. We stopped on our way here to see her. Here, I got a note for you. He dug a wadded piece of paper from his pocket and threw it toward Dwight.

Dwight, against his better judgment, picked it up and uncrumpled it. The handwriting was unmistakably his mother's.

Be kind, Be careful, the note said. Dwight walked to the door and opened it to the street. Go, he said. I can't believe you went to see mom, strung out. With that woman.

She wondered why you didn't come to see her last week, Darcy said. I think she was happy to see at least one of her sons.

Did you introduce her as your girlfriend? Your wife? Your crack buddy?

She had a car, man, Darcy said. And we needed gas money.

Dwight moved quickly across the room, narrowly missing the file boxes now, grabbing at the lapels of his own shirt on his brother. Darcy didn't resist, exactly, but he didn't do anything to move either. Dwight was straddling the table now, and wrapped his brother in a headlock, pulling him over on the couch, leaping on top of him, but still not getting him closer to the door. Darcy had at least a fifty pound advantage. Neither man spoke. They grunted. Dwight smacked his free fist into

Darcy's forehead. He wrenched at the head in his arm. Darcy finally moved. He stood up, hooking Dwight's leg with an arm, lifting both of them off the couch. He drove his weight forward. The two of them spilled over the coffee table, sent the boxes flying as they crashed to the floor. Darcy's head struck the floor with a solid thunk. His full weight fell onto Dwight as he slammed him down. Dwight's wind pushed out of his lungs with a guttural groan, and he released the headlock. The scuffle had lasted only seconds, but Darcy was breathing heavily as he raised himself to one knee. Dwight found his breath again with a sucking inrush of air. He was limp. Darcy leaned over and with an open hand slapped his face once, not really hard, a little more than a tap. A tap that said, I could break your jaw.

That's how people die, Darcy said. They over-commit to a half-assed move. Like a fucking one-arm headlock. They leave themselves open. They get winded or knocked down. And the knife comes out. Or the boots start to work. Or someone pulls a gun. Darcy was standing now. He rubbed his head where his hairline started. A red welt was forming there. I bet your hand hurts, he said. A punch to the top of the head. Fuck, what a loser.

Leave, Dwight said. It came out as a gasp.

I got no place to go, Darcy said. I'm staying in that room downstairs with the fucking Japanese mat. I got the key from the flowerpot. The flowerpot. What a fucking loser. Be like a fucking ghost. You just do whatever you do, and I'll do what I do.

Dwight spread his arms, laid his palms flat against the hardwood. He studied the whorls in the ceiling, where fifty years ago some new Canadian from Italy had trowelled plaster and swept it into curves and peaks. Futon. It's called a futon, Dwight said.

What is it you do with your days, Darcy said. Since you lost your job.

Risk management, Dwight said to the ceiling.

I never wanted to hurt you, he said. I just didn't want to hurt you. Who was she, I said. I don't even know her name. Who was she. I took another drink. The quinine suddenly tasted like bile. Lance rocked Darcy, then cradled him in one arm and with the other grabbed his drink and swallowed it down in a gulp. Who was she, I said again. Who was she? I threw my drink at him, in his direction. It missed him by two feet. The tall glass sailed past him over the rail and into the ocean. Was she a nurse too? Or was she a sweet young thing like Betty, a colleague's daughter? Was she the waitress in the diner? My voice was rising. He just sat there. I swore at him. I used all the words I had ever learned growing up in a mill town. I called him every vile name I could dream of. I was determined not to cry, but I did, eventually. Finally he spoke. Her name was Dorothy. Yes she was a nurse. She was older than he was. Her husband had died in the war, somewhere in the Pacific, on a submarine. He told me—for the only time he ever spoke about it—what it was like to work as an army surgeon, the things he had seen after D-Day, after the Battle of the Bulge. He said coming back from the war he took the first job that came his way, in Cleveland. Dorothy and he were both wrecks. They stayed drunk for a week after they met, and married a week later. She couldn't have babies, he said. And then there were other girlfriends. Lots of them. And drinking. But I'm different now, he said. You changed me, he said.

9.

A Cubic Foot of Cherries

8 July 1999

The last time his brother finds him is the very day he discovered the scorecard. Always ten years ago, always ten years later. Like a comet or a meteor. Dwight is forty then. He has been living out east, going to school. The summer he finds the scorecard and Darcy finds him, Dwight has been back in Seep, doing research. He is determined to complete his graduate program in library sciences. To finish his research project of the oral history of the day he was born. He is sober. He hasn't placed a bet of any kind since — he always claims he can't remember — but he knows very well. He bought a lottery ticket on his thirty-sixth birthday, and made a bet with himself: if he won any amount — $10; $66.54; $4000; $12 million — he would quit gambling. He matched four numbers. $66.54. Can't welch a bet, he thought to himself. Four years. That summer he is forty, he is staying at his fiancée (soon to be his third wife, he thinks then) Sara's parents' house, the Smithsons, in Cougarspaw, an unincorporated exurb just outside the city. Before it all crashes down that summer, before Darcy shows up burning rings with a crack pipe in the upholstery of a pickup truck, before Sara comes out with Julee, before the fire that time, he has been — content.

He wakes up early in the Smithsons' guesthouse on their acreage.

He makes notes and plans for his project as he drinks coffee and watches the morning light change the shapes of the foothills and mountains to the west. He cooks eggs and goes for walks in the coulee. Most days he climbs into his rattletrap Mazda GLC and angles over the twisty highway 1A, avoiding the limited access and divided Trans-Canada. Many days are bright and sunny as he points the car towards Seep, but even on the cloudy, or rainy, or foggy days, even on the morning of a freakishly late June snow squall, he is content.

He interviews Laugh Jack and Mike Kowalski, the only two left in town. He reads back issues of the Seep newspapers, and the newspapers from towns around Seep, and the company archives, in the Glenbow Archives in the city. He makes a trip to Lloydminster to interview Cody "Farmboy" Cody. He carries on a fractured correspondence with Luis Santiago's cousins in Miami, in broken English and Spanish. He drives one day to Regina to visit Alex in a nursing home, a futile trip. Alex can hardly recall Seep, let alone a baseball riot, and keeps wanting to show Dwight his hemorrhoids. He turns around and drives back, getting as far as Maple Creek before fatigue makes him stop and get a motel room. Every second Sunday he drives to Crowsnest Pass, up and down that sweep of road at the head of the Waldron community pasture, and sits with his mother, who passes him cryptic notes, and who one Sunday gives him a box with his baby book, the clippings from the newspaper describing the day he was born. He presses her with questions, and she refuses to answer. She passes a note: someday I will try to remember.

New Seep is almost dead. The house he will eventually see coming at him down the highway is already boarded up, along with most of the others on the company side of town. Laugh Jack has closed his barbershop. Across the river, Old Seep is hardly better. The general store there still opens for business every day but Sunday, but it sees little custom. Thirteen students are registered at the elementary school. The hotel burned down for the last time the winter before, and now folks go east to Caxton or west to Malcolm for glasses of draft beer.

Dwight talks to Sara every night — she is working on her own project in Ontario, amassing an amateur hockey archive of Belleville and environs. He is making progress with his first wife Sandi, who has changed her name to Esther, and who lives with a loosely organized collective of evangelical Christians in Hamilton. His daughter, Julee, from whom he has been estranged, agrees to come out to see him in Calgary. His son Dylan, from his second marriage, lives in France with his mother and her billionaire new husband. Julee is fourteen. She will fly out with Sara. They will come to the Calgary Stampede, The Greatest Outdoor Show on Earth. He will buy Julee an iconic flat-crowned Stampede black hat. They will watch the parade. They will go to the midway.

The logistics are complex. Sandi — now Esther — refuses to talk to him on the telephone. From what he can gather, she doesn't use the telephone, period. For anything. He doesn't even have a telephone number for her. Or a street address. So they communicate the old-fashioned way, by letter. His letters (and his support payment cheques, drawn from his student loans and scholarship money) go to a post office box. Over a matter of weeks, letters pass back and forth between Sandi-now-Esther, Dwight, Sara, and Julee. Sandi-now-Esther agrees to meet Sara at the Hamilton airport. He purchases a ticket in Julee's name and mails it to the PO box. Dwight understands, though it is never stated, that Sandi-now-Esther will surveil Sara at the airport; then, once they meet, further evaluate her. He knows there is a chance that Julee will not get on the plane. He is thankful that Sara is "normal" — conservative in dress, reserved, a listener more than a talker; that she is not flashy nor brassy. She doesn't have pierced ears. She believes in God. He worries her lapsed Catholicism might pose a problem if Sandi-now-Esther chooses to interrogate Sara's beliefs when they meet.

Julee and Sara are to arrive the evening before the parade that kicks off the Stampede, The Greatest Outdoor Show on Earth. That morning, Dwight makes the trip into Seep. He has started to enter some of the abandoned houses and buildings there. Many still have furniture in the rooms and dishes in the cupboards. He manages to unstick the window sash of the long low Quonset that had for decades called itself the smallest curling rink in the world. Dwight squirms through the window. The rink has a single sheet of ice, not quite regulation size. The last winter anyone made ice was decades ago. A series of circles on the concrete slab mark where the trout ponds were installed for the fish-farming escapade. They don't look big enough to sustain aquatic life. And in a pile of papers dumped in a corner of the administration office, along with years of club memberships, maintenance records pencilled on index cards, bonspiel posters (for bonspiels, they would make outdoor sheets to complement the one sheet inside), and other bric-a-brac, he finds the scorecard.

Two sheets of paper, one for the home team, one for the visitors. The papers are held together by a straight pin. The names of the players are listed. He discovers Luis Santiago wore number 32; Farmboy Cody wore 44. The umpire is listed as Hendrick Stroh — that is how he finds out "Hinky" was a nickname. The paper is blemished and creased, the indelible pencil used for scoring is faded and unreadable in one or two instances. But he can see the progress. The score was 3-2 for the Cubans in the bottom of the fourth, the last complete inning. Farmboy Cody had walked six and struck out four. Santiago had driven in all three Cuban runs. They had played one-third of the top of the fifth. Luis Santiago was the clean-up hitter, batting fourth in the lineup for the Cubans. He was the third batter up for the Cubans in the inning. The first batter struck out. The second hit a triple. The card shows Santiago advancing to first: HB. Hit batsman. His fielder's choice out at second is not marked. The record ends there. HB. In a spidery pencil, someone has written in the margin:

> August 16, 1959
> Seep Tournament Final
> No Decision
> Game Called on Account of Riot

When he gets back to Sara's parents' house, he removes the pin and spreads the scorecards on the table. There is evidence of past mildew, and stains where the paper has been wet, but the pages are now dry and brittle. He uses a pastry brush to work off any loose materials, then wipes the leaves with soft dry cloths. He sniffs the paper — a faint trace of mustiness, but nothing pungent. Dwight puts each page in the microwave, heating them in thirty second shots one at a time, then letting them cool, and nuking them again. He puts the sheets in their own plastic protective sleeves and then slides these into another just a bit bigger, wraps the straight pin in plastic wrap and drops it in too. He affixes a label to the sleeve, and files it in his carefully catalogued archive. He writes the number and a description on an index card, and files it away too. It is the last day Dwight formally maintains his archive.

Darcy always finds him. That day ten years ago, he is sitting in the den of the Smithson guest house, using the time before he drives to the airport to type up the transcript of the interview he has done with Laugh Jack a few days before. Sara calls from the Hamilton airport. She and Julee are almost boarding. He hears the strain in her voice.

It's a bit weird, Sara says.

How weird, Dwight asks.

Just — weird, Sara says. Julee's OK. She just is — somewhere else.

She's not with you, Dwight says.

No, she's here. But, she's playing at the kid's activity centre. Like, the one for toddlers.

Oh, Dwight says.

She seems happy. She doesn't say much, Sara says.

How was Esther, Dwight says. He can hear in his voice the scare quotes he puts around her name.

Actually, that's the other weird thing. Esther was great. I mean, really great, Sara says. She was just like — a normal mom.

Really, Dwight says. He hears a truck pull up. It honks twice.

Really, Sara says. Listen, they're going to call the flight. See you in a few hours?

Yes, Dwight says.

OK. I think we need to take this slow, Sara says. Like I don't know how fast Julee will adapt. Or whatever. To the Stampede. To you. Being away. Or whatever.

OK.

Dwight?

Yes, Dwight says. He is looking out the window. A large four-door truck, with big tires and a tonneau cover on the bed, is idling in the driveway. Tinted windows mask the interior. Dwight has a lump in his gut.

I love you. See you soon.

Yes, Dwight says. Me too, you too. The horn honks again. Sara hangs up on her end.

By the time he gets to the truck, he knows it's Darcy. The driver's window rolls down a crack. I found you, you little piss-ant, Darcy says. Get in. Dwight gets in. Let's go for a drive, Darcy says. They do.

You gotta try some of these cherries, Darcy says, reaching his hand to the back seat as he bounces the Dodge out of the Smithson's compound, riding over the painted white stones that mark the edge of the road, pulling onto the range road without slowing or looking. He hauls a fistful of fruit from a one-cubic-foot box lined with a garbage bag, and starts to pop them in his mouth. He lowers the window and machine-gun pits toward the road. Half of them stay in the truck. The dashboard to the left of the steering wheel, the driver's door armrest, the floor at Darcy's feet are marked with bits of pulp and cherry stones.

The best fucking cherries. Osoyoos cherries, Darcy says.

What do you want, Dwight says.

What a question, Darcy says. I want it all, man. Isn't that what everyone wants? All of it. He spits another cherry pit out the window.

What do you want right now, here.

More, please, from the free pile, Darcy says. I had an old lady who said that all the time. More from the free pile.

Her name is Amy, Dwight says.

What's that? Darcy has reached the highway. He slows this time, but still swings onto the Trans-Canada without stopping. He hits the gas hard.

Amy. It was Amy who used to say that. "Your old lady," who is the mother of your child.

You are wound up tight, Darcy says. My little bro's got a bug up his ass.

This is useless. Take me home, Dwight says. Darcy presses the gas pedal down further. God damn you are an ass.

They drive in silence for a few seconds, but it seems too much for Darcy.

Check this out, Darcy says. I got a disc player in this baby. A C fucking D. With a million watts of amp.

He cranks the stereo, sings along to Nirvana for a while. The truck pounds with the sound. Darcy drives faster. He presses the eject button. He yanks the CD from the player and hucks it out the window. Fuck that junkie shit, he says. He launches into a rambling near-incoherent story about how he acquired a cubic-foot box of cherries and how good they are they taste good and are good for you and he is proof positive that man can live on cherries alone. He slows at the Sibbald Trail turnoff, fishtails around the exit loop and speeds down a gravel road that leads into the woods. After a couple of kilometres he brakes hard and turns onto a rutted track that leads into the trees. Dwight has his head cranked hard to the right, refusing to look at his brother. He rolls the window back up.

Here we are, man. Wilderness adventure. Let's get wild. Darcy reaches into the console between them and fishes around until he finds what he is looking for — a glass tube, stained with resin, a piece of blackened pot-scrubber stuffed in one end as a filter, and a crack torch.

Dwight watches him now. Darcy's long cherry-stained fingers. Those hands that forever want to take over whatever happens to be in your hands — to do the task you struggle with, to tie the fishing line, to assemble the carburetor, to chop the wood, to swing the stick. Nails grimed, knuckles scabbed, the hands callused from the doing, the doing, the doing of things.

Darcy pulls a dirty white rock from a shirt pocket and rolls it expertly between that expert forefinger and thumb. He drops the rock into one end of the crack stem, and in a single practiced motion sweeps the torch from his lap, clicks it to ignite, raises the flame to the rock. The flame is a dry desert, hot like a miniature sun. The iceberg rock begins to glow. It melts. It turns to vapour. Darcy works the stem, rotating it, sucking the smoke, flicking the lighter on and off.

Do you remember when you set fire to the neighbourhood every week after the Boy Scouts meeting, Dwight says. The rock sizzles, releases its vapour. Darcy extinguishes the lighter and inhales deeply. He lets his breath out softly, so the smoke emanates from his lips and nostrils.

Finally Darcy says, No. I don't remember.

He shifts his torso, slouches his back against the door, twisting so his knee somehow finds room under the steering wheel, draping his arm over the headrest. The A/C blasts cold air into the cab of the truck. Darcy moves his hand from the headrest, tests the lighter one, two, three times, then puts it to the pipe again. He waves the flame at the bowl and sucks. Man, this lighter really cooks this shit, Darcy says.

I can't save you, Dwight says.

Darcy tilts his head, blows smoke at the roof of the cab. A brown muck stains the fabric there, testament to a thousand exhalations, ten thousand. The stain looks rougher or older than the rest of the roof. A constellation of interlocking burnt brown rings, like fish-scales or chain mail, stretches across the dome of the cab. Darcy touches the hot glass of the crack stem to the fabric. It marks it like a branding iron, adding another fish scale to the collection. He clicks the lighter on and off, on and off.

Nobody's asking to be saved, Darcy says. I'm not asking to be saved. I just need a place to get away from — to get away. He clicks the lighter. On. Off. On. Off. He is like the portrait of Dorian Gray — not the character Gray, but the portrait, growing older as Dwight looks on. Another click. The flame steady to the remnant of the rock, a wisp of a toke. He begins to rock his head, ever so slightly.

How can I trust you, Dwight says. After everything.

Darcy waves his hand like a shrug, like a maybe, like a yes, like a no, those expert fingers making a sign that fails to signify certainty. He lifts the lighter — stops — turns suddenly to face the front. The window rolls down, and Darcy tosses the crack stem into the woods. I'm fucked up, he whispers. That's my last rock.

How have you changed? I said. I had stopped crying. He was crying now. The whistle blew across the inlet. Shift change. How have you changed? You still drink. You're still getting girls pregnant and aborting the fetuses. You wanted me to abort Darcy. How have you changed? We have him now, he said. It's all different. I'm different. Betty and Margaret — it's all done. I fixed it. We can fix this. Darcy was asleep now, and Lance suddenly thrust him at me. I took the baby and Lance knelt in the narrow space of the cockpit. We can start again, he said. We can go somewhere new, the three of us. Please, Ellie. Please, give me this chance. He wept at my knees. We stayed like this for a long time. The wind picked up a bit, and the boat rocked. Eventually he crawled into the cabin and got the bottle and started to drink. Eventually the sun sank. I drove the boat back home. Lance was asleep on the floor of the cabin and I left him there.

10.

Turn Landscape into Asset

mid-June 2009

Dwight in the middle of a baseball diamond at Seep was both *in medias res* and *ab ovo*. It had been his idea. To hold the press conference there.

The Coalition for Assured Responsible Development — CARD — had sprung up to resist the redevelopment of New Seep. As with many such grassroots organizations that coalesce around a cause, its membership was lumpy. Country-mouse ranchers concerned about the dilution of the tax base and therefore their political clout in the municipal district. City-mouse environmentalists devoted to preserving what was left of watersheds and rare orchid habitats. A cadre of hoodie-wearing anticapitalist veterans of Seattle and Quebec City. A handful of the First Nations-reserve folks who detected the whiff of corruption in the collusion of the band with the developer. A different handful who resisted the continuing urbanization of reserve and adjacent lands on philosophical grounds. A geologist-turned-spiritualist who believed the convergence of the rock formations responsible for the falls was a site of cosmic energy. And Dwight. Willow had called him a few days after the meeting where he posed as Jon Andersson. You need to join us, Willow said.

Who's us? Dwight said.

We don't think we need another resort town, she said. Look what's happened to Malcolm. It's turning the whole valley into a theme park. Wilderness Disney. Real people can barely afford to live here.

Don't you live in Malcolm, Dwight said.

Uncle Dwight, Willow said. You grew up in Seep. This is a billion-dollar development. A billion dollars will wreck whatever is there.

It's already wrecked, Dwight said. What can we do.

Stop it, Willow said.

The first meetings were in the community halls like Birdwing's, scattered across the foothills, and libraries in Caxton and Malcolm. The group managed to come to consensus on a mission statement: To stop development at the Seep townsite. But they got hung up on vision and values. The anarchists (and some of the First Nations) advocated direct action. Some of the environmentalists wanted studies and legislative intervention. Some of the environmentalists wanted structured parklands. Some of the ranchers wanted access to water. Some of the ranchers (and some of the First Nations) wanted compensation. The geologist wanted meditation. Dwight wanted.

Work at the site proceeded. The developers did not have approval from the Sheepshorn Municipal District for the Area Structure Plan, which was the first step to massive terraforming, infrastructure, and condo pre-sales. But they could go ahead with the work that fell broadly under the rubric of demolition. All the sound houses were sold and moved to a house recycler in Cayley. Those that were not salvageable were bulldozed. Pits were dug, searching for forty-five-gallon drums full of PCBs and creosote and other assorted contaminants abandoned before waste management became an integral part of industrial development. The search bore fruit. Truckloads of drums were shipped to the Alberta Special Waste Treatment Facility in Swan Hills, and several areas were cordoned off where pits were dug and remediation begun.

At the gatherings, Dwight sat and listened. When the meeting was called to order, they began with an acknowledgement that they were in the traditional territory of a First Nation. Dwight would take a seat close to the back of whatever room they were in and pull out a newspaper. As someone wrote an agenda on a flip chart, using different coloured markers to indicate different priorities, he studied the morning-line odds on the baseball games and picked his Sports Select numbers. If there was a vote or a show of hands requested, he tried to cast his lot with whichever side seemed the majority.

After the meetings, he sometimes had a coffee with Willow and some of her friends. Willow had been in Montreal for a few years, first studying, then working on community action projects. She was not quite thirty, but experienced in organizing people to fight the system. When my mom told me what was happening here, I decided I had to come back, she said one day.

What does she make of all this. I mean, Amy is working for the other side, Dwight said. Dwight hadn't told Willow that her father — Darcy — was in Calgary. He hadn't told Amy, either.

Willow shook her head, sipped her green tea. Oh, Uncle Dwight. She's a fifty-year-old woman who needs a job. I can't blame her. She doesn't have a choice, Willow said.

Just call me Dwight, OK? "Uncle" sounds weird.

Willow smiled.

What do the developers think? Dwight said. Of you and your mom. Her working for them. You working against.

I think they hope she'll give them information, Willow said.

Do you think she will? Dwight said.

There's nothing they don't already know, Willow said. Somebody at these meetings is bound to be reporting to them. There's some folks wondering if you're on their payroll.

Me, Dwight said. Why would they think I'm working for them.

Because you never say much, Willow said. Just sit back there reading newspapers, writing in a little book. I told them you were my uncle, you were from Seep.

Dwight sipped a coffee, resisted the urge to pull out his notes and double-check the over-under on tonight's MLB games.

We've got to be transparent, Willow said. That's how to win at this. They're the ones with all the secrets. Don't worry, I know you're not a spy. Somebody might be, but not you.

The idea for the picnic came up when someone said CARD needed to gain some attention from the media.

One morning, in the Kraft Foods Community Meeting Centre at a food superstore in a suburban power centre in Calgary, Dwight couldn't hide at the back. As people were settling in, Willow said, Let's put the chairs in a big circle today. She looked right at him, and said, Uncle Dwight, can you help us set up? He folded his paper and slipped it into his satchel. He had nearly $22,000 in the inside pocket of his jacket. He had been on a roll for the last couple of days, couldn't lose at anything. I could just walk out, he thought. He took a seat between a young white man with dreadlocks tucked in a tam, smelling of body odour and marijuana, and a genial white-haired woman with knitting in her lap. Am I a cliché, too, he wondered.

A man from the Watershed Conservation Keepers and a woman from the Wilderness Foundation talked about the articles they had posted on their websites, and the email campaigns they'd started. Willow gave a précis of the media reporting — the two daily papers in Calgary were playing it very straight, she said, balancing their stories between reporting the regulatory process of land planning, grabbing sound bytes from those pro and con. There had been an article featuring an interview with one of the band councillors who stressed the need for First Nations economic self-sufficiency. Peter Larkin, who wrote a breezy businessman-about-town column, had been wildly enthusiastic for the development; Martha Givens, the token liberal for the tabloid, had blasted it. Willow was quoted a couple of times on behalf of CARD. But they never mention these meetings, Willow said. We need to devise a strategy.

Forget the lame-ass media, the dreadlocked tam guy said. Make our own. Jordan and I already got a YouTube channel going. We be the media.

I know the river and wilderness people have a website, but do we have one, Dwight said. Everyone at the meeting looked at him. They had forgotten he was there.

Websites are so yesterday, dude, dread-tam said.

Great question, Willow said. Yes, we do.

Do we push anything out on it, Dwight asked.

Not exactly yet, Willow said. Are you volunteering?

I'm not really a PR guy. Or a tech guy. But if the page is already set up, and someone else is making content, I can probably get stuff posted and emailed out to media. Put links to your YouTube on it, he said, turning to the young man.

Facebook, man, the young man said, shaking his dreadlocks. And this Twitter thing.

What's that, Dwight said.

Social media, dude, the young man said. Websites are for dinosaurs.

Good point, Jared, Willow said. She turned to the flip chart and wrote: Dwight — Webmaster. Jordan & Jared — Social Media Experts.

Not experts, Jared said. Guerrillas. Social Media Guerrillas. Willow nodded and started to speak. No, really, Jared said. Change it. On the board. Guerrillas.

The group started to talk about how to catch the attention of the general public. None of the television stations had covered the story yet. Jared kept rolling his eyes.

As they spoke, Dwight was calculating how he was going to be able to juggle his time. The money in his jacket felt like a brick of plutonium.

We could have a picnic and a press conference at Seep, Dwight said. He went on: at the old ball diamond. All the bulldozers are parked there. How it used to be the gathering place in the summer.

Everyone liked the idea, even Mr. Dreadlocks. The fact that it was an occupation of private property appealed to the anarchists and the First Nations activists. There was a bit of discussion whether the developers might try to force them to leave, but it was decided that an eviction would make good press. Let 'em try to stop us, Jared said. That'll make awesome video. The environmentalists planned a hike. The ranchers offered to bring beef. Someone else countered with vegan stew. It was decided: both. The folks from the reserve would erect a teepee and build a sweat. They set a date for mid-August. Saturday the fifteenth. The day before Dwight's fiftieth birthday.

Dwight volunteered to put together a history backgrounder for the website. I know a bit about that, he said. Later that night, after another short but winning run at roulette, he checked the developer website. They were extolling the history of the area as a marketing tool:

> The unique geography of Seep begins sixty-five million years ago, when the forces of nature pushed the great plains under the older rock to the west, to thrust up the Rocky Mountains. The exposed ridges and outcrops that formed the falls at Seep are the legacy of that great upheaval.

Dwight admired the succinct compression of several million years of plate tectonics into two sentences. He knew from his own research that the outcropping and faults at the site were not unique to Seep, but that their exposure there was a particularly good example of the meeting of the Cardium Formation anticline of the plains with the Front Ranges of the mountains.

The website played up the connection to the First Nations —
"Before the arrival of the Europeans, the First Peoples of the area
inhabited the Bow River corridor for thousands of years." This was
technically correct. But the archaeological record indicated that the
actual site where the town stood saw little or no sustained occupation.
The very geography that marked the distinctiveness of the place made
it hard to live on. The cliffs made access to water difficult. The rocky
outcroppings were a poor source of forage for game. The Big Horn
Sheep, namesakes of the Sheepshorn Municipal District, tended to the
higher slopes upriver, and the shale and scrub didn't attract deer and
elk. The pre-European activity occurred a few miles upstream and
downstream in the various flats and meadows around the river. The
developer website continued: "The First Peoples welcomed the first
European to visit: David Thompson, two hundred years ago." But
Thompson didn't linger, and the developer didn't quote the cryptic
notes from his journals: "November 1800: The falls here 10 or 15 ft.,
and rapids. Banks are some 200 ft. in parts. Portage of a 1000 yds. to cut
across point. There is enough water for large canoes fully loaded even
at this time of season." Thompson was on foot — but his surveyor's
eye was for the navigation of watercraft and the transport of
commodity. Ultimately, the reaches of the Bow were to play little role
in the trade of furs.

"The Bow River was the sacred home territory of the people who
had lived there for generations, and Treaty 7 in 1877 bestowed the lands
to their nation." Yes, thought Dwight, the area was part of Treaty 7.
But he had his own interpretation. The rich meadows that abutted the
bottom of the falls and rolled eastward were excluded — the drafters
of the treaty foresaw the agricultural potential, and that narrow strip of
lands was excluded from the treaty. But the future site of New Seep itself had no value — too rocky for growing things, too rough for
dwellings. Stick it in the treaty. "The Canadian Pacific Railway acquired
a right of way through the area, and the falls became a favourite stop

for travellers — offering a gateway to the mountains themselves, and a picturesque rugged beauty oft-sketched by visitors on the way to Banff." Dwight liked that word: "acquired." Less than ten years after granting the land in the treaty, a ribbon of it was expropriated for the great Canadian pork barrel. And again: "1n 1908, Prairie Mountain Light & Power procured the thousand acres that comprise the area under consideration for redevelopment, in order to build the dams." He liked that word even more: "procured." He knew there were still some elders, whose fathers and grandfathers were alive when the procurement took place, who insisted that the purchase price was a dozen horses. The archives of PML&P were uncharacteristically vague on the political machinations of the transfer. There were letters from high profile Members of Parliament, a future Prime Minister, a future member of both the United Kingdom's war cabinet of the Great War and Churchill's World War II cabinet — clearly, powerful forces influenced how the land was "procured." He had located an order in council from the Department of Indian Affairs authorizing "the transfer of territory for considerations." He had found a title transfer document that recorded $10,000 as the purchase price. And indeed the money was distributed as a payment of $5 a head to the band; the balance was used to buy fifty broodmares. The band fought for years for the horses to actually be procured and the record of their delivery was ambiguous.

Since the 1930s, a series of legal challenges by the band had ebbed and flowed, gathering financial momentum since the 1970s, so that each successive half-decade added another zero to the claim. In the end, nearly six hundred of the thousand acres were sold back to the band for $1. The three hundred acres of the New Seep townsite itself were sold for $10 million to the present development interests. IHC — the successor to PML&P, still owned a hundred acres comprising the dam and utility sites. Dwight noticed that the website didn't mention the tent city that had been built in the early 1940s: a World War II internment camp — first for undesirable aliens, then occupied by German soldiers, until a more permanent location was constructed a few miles away in the mountains.

In his personal archive, he had a copy of a photograph of PML&P's initial conception for the site:

Its bluntness appealed to Dwight. Put dam there, it said. Build power plant here. Raise water to this line. Turn landscape into asset. He posted the photo on the CARD website.

Then he clicked the bookmark that linked to an online poker room.

We started over. What could I do? Go home to Squamish, and live in a hovel with a logger who would accept Darcy as long as I produced some heirs of his own? Came to Seep. Another company town. And for a couple of years, it was better. He drank. Oh how he drank. But he stayed home at nights, with me. For a couple of years. Then he didn't. He added gambling to his vices. And town politics. Those three were inseparable in Seep — politics, drinking, and gambling. I know you know something about that. The men gambled on anything. They played cards. They bet a hundred dollars on a coin toss. I never heard about abortions again. But I heard about the gambling. One day Lance comes home in Kenny Orlov's brand new Chrysler. Just as suddenly, it belongs to Alex. I heard about a man who lost a quarter section to one of the operators at the dam. He farmed it for twenty more years, paying rent. There were occasional thaws between us. After five years, I was pregnant again, with you. It wasn't an easy pregnancy. I was tired, anemic. Darcy was five or six, and a handful. He couldn't sit still. He broke every toy he got his hands on. Your father just stayed away. When he did come home, I was more likely to find him on the kitchen floor than in my bed.

11.

They Built a Deck

23-30 June 2009

One day, after a morning meeting at the Caxton library, Dwight arrived home just as a fire engine was pulling away from the front of his house. Darcy stood on the sidewalk, shirtless as usual, waving as the firefighters drove away. Helmut and Dagmar, his neighbours across the way, stood on their lawn, each holding a watering can, but frankly staring. The street retained a strong charred smell, and the hint of a smoky haze hung in the air. Dwight didn't even bother to speak to Darcy as he strode up the walk and through the open door to his house.

Man, those guys are good, Darcy was saying as he followed. Just all business. When they were inside, and out of earshot of Helmut and Dagmar, Dwight turned to face his brother.

What did you set fire to, Dwight said. He sniffed, but couldn't smell a fire in the house.

Darcy was waving a swatch of paper. They didn't give you a ticket. Just a fucking warning. Man, those guys were good.

Dwight walked through the house. Out the kitchen window, on the back lawn, a pile of blackened lumber smouldered. A big pile.

What is that? Dwight said.

Your deck was toast, Darcy said. Every fucking time I went out for a smoke — Boom! a foot goes through a board. Crack! Something splits. Look at this, Darcy said, and pulled off a shoe to reveal a nasty gash. A fucking nail did that.

Dwight walked out the back door and stumbled as he stepped over the threshold. The level was different than what he expected.

I just pulled the fucker up, Darcy said. Look at that shit. He walked to the edge of the pile, where an unburned deck board protruded. Dry rot. Did you build this thing? It looks like something you would build, Darcy said.

A garden hose snaked to the pile, where a steady stream of water continued to quench the embers. The lawn was soggy with muddy soot, and getting soggier.

Look at this, Darcy said. It was built right over this old fucking patio. And on the grass. Just laying there. No posts. No anchors. Just a bunch of wood stacked on the ground. No wonder it was fucking rotten.

You burned the deck, Dwight said. You destroyed it, then you set fire to it.

Man, you don't want to be paying for hauling this shit away, Darcy said. But it's all good. The fire dudes just gave you a warning.

Gave *me* a warning? Dwight said.

I convinced them that I'd put it out, Darcy said. I know all about this stuff. If they'd used the hose and the pumper, huge fucking bill and a fine. But it's all under control. Let's build you a deck, little bro.

They built a deck. Darcy did most of the building. Dwight's major contribution was to pull out his wallet at Home Depot, to rent and drive the truck to transport the lumber, posts, hardware and bags of cement, and to lift and tote. He got a post hole auger and a small cement mixer from Randall's Rental World, took those back and exchanged them for a portable table saw and two heavy-duty cordless drills. Darcy knew what he was doing. He drew up plans with a ruler and pencil, made estimates for materials. The new deck was nearly half again as big as the old one. He convinced Dwight to splurge on composite deck boards over cedar or pressure-treated lumber. No maintenance, ever.

The old concrete patio, which had been hidden by the old deck, presented a challenge. If I had my druthers, Darcy said, I'd jackhammer the whole fucking thing. but that's the Cadillac fix, and we can settle for the Chevy.

Dwight heard his father's words there — *If I had my druthers* was one of his turns of speech — but he chose to ignore it.

The Chevy solution was to break holes through the patio where they needed to auger for the footings. Another trip to Randall's for a jackhammer. At the end of two days, they had poured the footings. Post anchors were set in the concrete. A matrix of neat lines of twine stretched from stake to stake to mark where the beams would go. Tomorrow we break this bastard's back, Darcy said.

Night fell. They sat on lawn chairs in a corner of the yard. Darcy had fashioned a portable firepit from a galvanized washtub that had held an herb garden five or six summers ago. They used pieces of the old deck for fuel, but kept the fire a manageable size. They roasted hot dogs on the end of straightened coat hangers, waiting for the wood to subside to a bed of embers. Gottta make sure the paint and the pressure-treated shit is burned up good before we cook, Darcy said. For two days, Darcy had talked non-stop. For two days. About decks and fences he had built for rich people on the West Coast. A house he had helped with on Mayne Island, where they had to hack a road through the forest to the highest point on the island, an outcropping of bare rock overlooking the ocean. They flew the fucking roof beams in on a helicopter, he said. About fights he had witnessed at biker bars in Washington state. About fights he had been in while working as a bouncer in a strip club on Davie in Vancouver. About driving a stolen Camaro to Fairbanks,

Alaska, selling it there, and stealing a Firebird to drive home and sell in Port Coquitlam. He drank no-name beer and cremated the cans in the fire, tossing in chain-smoked cigarette butts as tombstones.

Where do you get your money, Dwight asked.

Darcy stopped talking. Then said: none of your fucking business.

For beer and smokes, Dwight said.

Curiosity killed the cat, Darcy said, stretching out "curiosity," enunciating each syllable.

You show up in my front room, claiming to be broke. Needing gas money. And suddenly every time I go out and come home you've got a box of beer and a carton of cigarettes. That's not curiosity, Dwight said.

A nose-sticker. You were always a fucking nose-sticker, Darcy said. He drained the beer he was drinking, crushed the can and tossed it in the fire.

It's my house, Dwight said.

You got any pistachios? Darcy said. We oughtta get a big bag of pistachios, one of those burlap sacks of the suckers. You ever burn a mess of pistachio shells? You load an empty can full of 'em, and throw 'em into a bed of coals like this. It starts smoking, like a steam engine under a full head. Just gushing this crazy-ass white smoke. Fucking rank, white smoke, smells like burning dog crap. Then all of a sudden, poof, the smoke catches fire and a green jet of flame shoots out the can, like a fucking torch. A pistachio green torch.

I have a right to know, Dwight said.

You have a right to know fuck all, Darcy said. I don't ask you about your shit. I don't care if you fuck off without a word till all hours of the morning. I don't ask you why your eyes look like two peeholes in the snow after you stumble in at 4:00 AM. Your shit is your shit. Darcy hauled himself to his feet. Good night, he said and walked into the house.

Dwight watched the fire for a few minutes, then gathered the uneaten hot dogs and buns and Hawkins Cheezies and marshmallows and took them into the house. He stowed everything in the fridge and cupboards, closing the opened packages with plastic sealing clips, shutting the wieners in a Ziploc. He wiped the countertops, ran a sponge-mop over the kitchen floor, then washed his hands methodically at the kitchen sink. He went to his home office and checked the baseball scores. He had lost $200 on his main Sport Select plays, but his long-shot hedge bet was still in play. The Blue Jays were in extra innings in Oakland, a late game. He had a chance at $178. He stood in his living room, jangling his car keys in his pocket. He could hear Darcy snoring downstairs. *Two peeholes in the snow*. Another favourite turn of phrase from his father. Darcy snored like his father, too. Dwight went out the front door and drove to a casino.

On the day you were born, I could feel the contractions starting. It was hot hot hot. Everybody in town was in a lather over the baseball game. A lot of people were betting a lot of money. It was like a dance mania from the middle ages. People were drunk with betting. And they were drunk. Jim Peebles was taking the bets. The town cop. That says something about Seep. Tens of thousands of dollars — I never knew how much was bet in total, but I know it was more money than most people in town would see in ten years of working.

12.

Laugh Jack

15 July 1999 (16 August 1959)

Dwight recorded Laugh Jack's story in two parts. The first part was July 5, 1999, three days before Darcy, Sara, and Julee converged in his life. The second part was ten days later, July 15, 1999. The day Sara, Julee, and Darcy left his life. Sara, probably forever. Julee, he still had hopes he would see again. Darcy reappeared ten years later. On July 5, Dwight met Laugh Jack at his closed barbershop late in the afternoon. Jack was asleep in his chair. No customers today, Jack said. Just like the last couple of years I was open for business. They walked through the empty town and sat on Jack's porch and talked. That was the first interview.

This is a transcription of the second interview with Laugh Jack, of the tape that never was transcribed. Dwight arrived in Seep on a blustery day in mid-July. It felt more like winter. The temperature was barely above zero Celsius in the foothills near Seep, and the rain seemed determined to turn to snow. Darcy and Dwight's fiancée Sara and his daughter Julee had gone to Calgary to visit the Stampede fairgrounds. Dwight found Laugh Jack in his tiny company house, wrapped in a sweater and drinking tea and scotch. Dwight sorted his things out, pulled out a yellow legal pad and four pencils, and put the recorder on the coffee table between them. He pressed the RECORD button.

DE: Okay, this is Thursday, July 15, 1999. This is Dwight Eliot and I'm interviewing Jack Rees. This is a follow-up interview to the interview of July 5, 1999. The subject of the interview is the Seep baseball riot that occurred on August 16, 1959. The day I was born. Jack, last week we heard your story about how you arrived in Seep after the Second World War.

JACK: The company barber. Light and Power were hiring all sorts of folks. Barbers, grocers, plumbers. Doctors.

DE: You talked about how my parents arrived in the mid-1950s. Light and Power built the school, the clinic, a few store-fronts.

JACK: The goddamn high point of the whole town. They had the mine still going then up the side valley, in Lanyard Creek. All sorts of dam operators, millwrights, power linemen, the miners. Closed the mine in '54. Right after your mom and dad came. Then it was downhill.

DE: But we never got around to talking about the game.

JACK: No, I guess we didn't.

DE: That's what I'm here for. I want to get that story.

JACK: You've got that story ten ways from Sundays by now, haven't you?

DE: Not from you.

JACK: All those old men. Hinky Stroh. Peebles. All liars.

DE: Liars?

JACK: Afraid of their own shadows. What they might have done. What they don't know. What they forget.

DE: What did they do?

JACK: You talk to Alex, that bastard?

DE: Yes. It was a bit pointless. He doesn't have much memory left. Any memory, actually.

JACK: That bastard.

DE: You didn't like him.

JACK: What's there to like? Let me ask you something. You ever alone in a room with him?

DE: Me? Alex? No. I guess not.

JACK: You're lucky then.

DE: Was he —

JACK: A diddler. No. Never got caught. No one's come out of the woodwork to point a finger. Just whispers. Back then, whispers.

DE: I don't know what to say.

JACK: Don't say anything then.

DE: Is that why you won't talk about the day I was born? You don't want to say anything?

JACK: You're a terrible interviewer. Anybody ever tell you that? Gimme that goddamned blanket off the couch. And haul that electric fire closer. July and it's damn near snowing.

DE: Maybe I should come back another day. We seem to have got off on the wrong foot.

JACK: There won't be another day. I like you. As much as I like anybody. Your mother was — is — an amazing human being.

DE: You seemed close to my mother.

JACK: What're you getting at?

DE: This is a hard question to ask. Did you love my mother?

JACK: Go to hell. Your mother is better than all of us. What would she want with a broken-down bachelor like me.

DE: You always seemed to be around when I was growing up. After Lance died.

JACK: Didn't I already tell you to go to hell? She needed someone to look out for her, that was all. I was a friend.

DE: O.K.

JACK: None of your goddamned business.

DE: O.K.

JACK: Let's change the subject.

DE: O.K. What happened on August 16, 1959.

JACK: The circumstances of your birth. I guess you could say they were unusual. You're curious. You have an idea in your head. You think you know everything. Already. So you ask people about it. And they tell you what you want to hear. Now you're asking me.

DE: Jack. This all sounds ominous.

JACK: You go ahead and ask me something.

DE: O.K. Tell me about the day — the weather, the field, the people, whatever.

JACK: Oh, you've got all that. Sunny. Hot. Been dry for weeks. No rain. Dust. Everybody out for the day. Folks from Light and Power. Folks from across the bridge in the town proper. Indians. All the stupid shenanigans people get up to — sack races, three-legged races, tug-of-war. Some tin-can carnival outfit with the carousel, and a Ferris wheel no bigger than a combine. A popcorn kettle, spun sugar. A goddamn parade at noon. A beautiful fucking summer's day. And the goddamn baseball.

DE: It was a tournament — all weekend long.

JACK: That was just bullshit. Nobody from this part of the country could beat the Selects. Light and Power hired ringers to work at the dam and the mine. You know that. You've heard all that. Their job was to play. Hockey in the winter. Baseball in the summer. Boys from Iowa, Nebraska. Negroes from Texas and Georgia. A handful of Canadian boys. Farmboy Cody was one of them, a Canadian, plucked from the plough in Saskatchewan. Then goddamn if these Cubans don't show up. And they could play ball.

DE: How did the riot happen?

JACK: I'm trying to tell you a story here. The background.

DE: Were you at the game?

JACK: Everybody was at the game. I was keeping an eye on your mother.

DE: Where was my dad?

JACK: He was busy. Your mother was big as a house. Wearing a big white floppy hat like this. Trying to keep the sun off. She was sweating. And huffing.

DE: You're holding your hands up to show the hat was wider than the shoulders. I'm just saying that out loud because the tape recorder can't see your gestures.

JACK: Now I'm gonna drink some tea and blow my nose. You need that recorded too?

DE: Where was Darcy?

JACK: He was around. I think one of the moms had charge of him. A tight game. Kids like monkeys. But all the grown-ups was watching. Those Cubans were something. Crafty. Bunt singles. Stealing third. Loaded the bases every inning. Farmboy Cody's wild as hell. Walks three in a row in the second, then strikes out three to get out of the inning. The Selects needed a sharp double play in the third to keep it all tied up. The Cubans had this big slugger. Looked like maybe he was part Negro. The bat looked like a toothpick in his hands.

DE: Luis Santiago.

JACK: Sure. You got all the answers. He had a two-run homer in the first. Struck out swinging hard in the second. Farmboy struck out three in a row that inning with the bases loaded. Our boys squeaked out a couple of runs to tie it.

DE: I found the scorecard last week. It said the score was 3-2 when the game was called.

JACK: Do I look like I give a good goddamn about the scorecard? I'm telling you the score was tied.

DE: If you say so.

JACK: I say so. Top of the fifth. Tied. All hell breaks loose. Man on third. One out. Cody looking rattled. Your mother sitting beside me sweating. Groaning. This big Cuban gorilla comes to the plate. Simpson comes out to the mound. Arnie Simpson. He was the manager. Foreman of a crew. He was a ringer, too. From California. But he actually had a trade. Millwright. He's talking to Farmboy. It's obvious what to do. Walk the bastard. Set up the double play. Shut up now. You look like you're going to interrupt me. You just shut up now. I'm telling you a story. I don't see the next pitch. Your mom is moaning again. But I hear it. A smacking sound. Like a tenderloin of beef dropped on the tile floor. Smack. When I look over the Cuban is on the ground. But he's getting up. He's moving kind of slow, the way a big animal does when they stand up. Like a buffalo. Or moose. He's got one thing on his mind. He's going to tear Cody's arm off and beat him with it. More hell breaks loose. There's a big wrestle. There's a mob and nobody gets a punch off. Hinky Stroh is waving his mask around. Pointing at this guy and that guy. Nobody pays no mind. Everybody gets separated. Hinky makes a lot of threats, but he doesn't dare kick anybody out of the game. The Cuban gets it in the neck, just below the jaw, just above the collarbone. Which is lucky. Cause if he got it in the face, it would've broke his jaw or worse. Now he's got a lump on his neck like a goddamn goitre. And it's getting bigger. He takes first base. Next pitch, Farmboy throws a slider on the knuckles. This Cuban pulls it, a lazy two-bouncer down toward third. Double-play ball. It's close, a choppy, slow-moving ball. Third baseman's a lefty, he's got to pivot to make the throw. Why the hell they have a lefty at third, I don't know. Shoots a glance at the runner on third to keep him honest. He sidearms a rocket to second for the tag. But this Salazar —

DE: Santiago...

JACK: OK, if you say so. Santiago. He's coming on like gang-
busters. Remember I said he was like a buffalo. Now he's a
buffalo doing a drop kick. No pretending he's trying to slide.
He launches himself feet first at the man covering second.
Make no mistake. This Cuban is aiming for his can.

DE: Zosky. Eddie Zosky's on second.

JACK: Yeah. A beanpole Polack. I think he was from Minnesota,
if I remember. So the Polack tags up and gets the throw off
to first. He twists just enough. The Cuban's spikes come in
just above the knee. Sounded like a base hit. Snap. You
could hear the bone break. And then a holler. Polack's
rolling around on the ground, screaming like a stuck pig.
And the Cuban gets up, looks down at this guy. He kicks
dirt in his face. Like this. Insult to injury. If hell broke loose
before, I don't know what to call this. Worse hell. The
crowd is on its feet, spitting mad. The Cuban turns from
the poor fool on the ground, heads toward Cody on the
mound. Cody takes a step towards him. Has second
thoughts. The Cuban has murder in his heart. Cody turns
tail and starts running. Jackson, he's the Selects catcher. In-
tercepts the Cuban. Santiago, right? Tackles him, like
they're playing football, not baseball. They roll around.
Players pouring out of both dugouts. Men climbing down
out of the stands. Cody's still running. A couple of Cubans
have him boxed in an open patch of ground in shallow
right. Cody's picked up a bat somehow. Waving it around
like a goddamn sword. Like he's Errol Flynn. And there's
Stitch Washington comes up to one these Cubans from behind. Stitch has got a bat, too. Stitch was from the south —
Georgia. But he's been kicking around ball teams in Canada
for a long time. Last I heard, he lived in Winnipeg. Had a big

old family there, all athletes. One of his girls was in the
Olympics.

DE: She was a hurdler. Stitch died in '88.

JACK: OK. So Stitch comes up and clobbers a Cuban in the back
of the head. Didn't really hear this one. Too much noise. But
we saw it. You could hear everybody, like suddenly a collective Oh! from the crowd. Like you see on TV nowadays, when
a golfer just misses a putt. Oh! The Cuban drops like a sack
of rocks. The other Cuban kneels down to check his buddy.
Stitch freezes for a second. Then starts to run. Across the
field. Over the right-field fence. And half the Cubans stop
fighting in the infield and chase after. Let me tell you, it was
something. I was in Belgium in the war. And what I saw on
the baseball diamond looked like a fucking battlefield. Someone had driven a Light and Power panel van where they were
loading the Polack. The Cuban with the smashed head is sitting up. Uniform looks like an abattoir apron. He's bleeding
from his head, from his nose and mouth. Men are spitting
streams of bloody tobacco juice from split lips. You can see
where they've turned their heads to wipe their mouths on
the shoulders. Their jerseys are reddish brown.

DE: Where's my dad? What's going on with me and my mother?

JACK: You wanted the story. I'll get to it. On the mound, a meeting of the brain trust. This Sugarcane Sanchez, or whatever
his name is, is talking. Spanish and English. The welt on his
neck is about the size of a pineapple. Already turning blue.
Our manager, Simpson, is chewing a cigar. Hinky Stroh is
looking at his scorecard or in the goddamn rule book. Jim
Peebles is there in his goddamn red tunic and Mountie Stet-
son. Got his hand resting on his goddamn gun and I figure
that's to keep his finger out of his nose. As you might sur-
mise, I think that bastard was a waste of skin.

DE: So where's my dad?

JACK: Ah yes, the good doctor. Your dad's there too, with his doctor bag.

DE: Helping the wounded.

JACK: Nope. Standing on the mound.

DE: He couldn't help with my mom — with me. He was looking after the injured. Negotiating the end of the hostage incident.

JACK: If you say so. I can't speak for your father. Wouldn't want to. Don't really know what he was doing. But he was on the mound with the rest of the nabobs.

DE: What were you doing? Where were you in all this?

JACK: Your mother. Just about the time Stitch brained the Cuban. I was standing up. All of a sudden, she lets out a scream of her own. Calls to your father. Lance! She grabs my arm. I had bruises for weeks where she clutched at me. Lance! she hollers. She's standing bent over as best as a pregnant woman who's about to deliver can bend over. There's a puddle at her feet. On the plank of the grandstand. It's all happening now. She's gasping. Somehow I got her off the grandstand. We weren't very high up in the bleachers, thank god for that. I got her around back of the seats where there was a little shade. Just hold on, I told her. I'll go get Lance. The baby's coming now, she screamed. It's coming now. I snuck a look onto the field. Your dad was with a delegation that was marching out of the diamond. Peebles, Alex the bastard. Stroh. Simpson. The Cubans. I grabbed a kid who was catching flies with his open mouth. Run and tell the doc his wife is having her baby. The kid stood there. Go on, you little shit, I said. Which one is the doc, he said. The one with the little black bag, you dunce. I gave him a swift kick in the ass and go back to your mom. She's on the ground now. There's a bunch of Indian women around her. Someone had the sense to put that goddamn great hat of hers under her. Now you'd figure that some of these Indians might know something about midwifery. I don't know how much help they had birthing their babies, at least before your dad arrived in town. But Jesus Christ. There she was huffing and pushing and she still had her goddamn drawers on. Lady, push, one of them said. No, I said. Not yet. Your mother was between contractions. Fact is, I was trained as a medic in the army. Told you that last week. And fact is, I had helped catch a baby before. Twice. In Holland. Now I'd had decent help there. One time there was an army doc there, and another time a Dutch midwife. So I wasn't entirely swimming upstream. Damnedest thing. Get me some goddamned boiling water, I say and an Indian says OK and wanders off. I get her drawers off. Your mom heaves into another contraction. And goddamned if I don't see the top of your head. Take it easy, Ellie, I say. Go to hell, she says. Where's Lance? Go to hell, she says again. Just hold on, I say. The spasm stops. Hold her hand, I say to another one of the ladies and she does. Breathe now, I say. Catch your breath. The other Indian lady comes back with a billycan full of boiling water. I was just making tea, she says. I brought a first-aid kit too, she says. I rip open a pack of dressing, dunk it in the can and scrub my hands as best I can. I'm thinking ahead, and I drop my jack-knife I carry in my pocket into the can too. Throw in a another pack of dressing. Know I'll need it later. Here, I still got that knife.

DE: Just for the record, Jack. You're showing me a bone-handled folding-clasp knife.

JACK: That's right. My father gave it to me when I was a boy.

DE: And that's the knife you used to cut my umbilical cord.

JACK: Getting ahead of the story. But yes. Used the knife to cut the cord. But that's a bit later. Ellie starts to grunt again. One look and I figure this is it. Push, I say. C'mon Ellie, push. She howls. She screams. And dear lord, she pushes. I've got my hand under your head, then your shoulders slide out and I know we're home free. She pushes again and you slip into the world. Before I can do anything like hold you up and slap your behind, you give a little cough. I can see you take a deep breath. And then you cry. You were one healthy-looking little boy. Pink as bubble gum. Crying to beat the band. Wiggly right off the bat. I pass you to your mom and she cradles you to her chest. As best she can. The cord's still attached. And she hasn't delivered the afterbirth.

DE: Placenta. Sounds better.

JACK: I checked the cord. As I'm holding it, it stops pulsing. Fished the knife from the billycan, cut a couple of strips of gauze from the boiled dressing. Tied off the cord. Cut it.

DE: Wow. With this knife.

JACK: Wow is right. You should feed her, one of the Indians says. He, your mom says. He's a little boy. You're crying. Your mom unbuttons her dress, and gives you her breast. Then she delivers the placenta right away. Let me tell you, I was thankful for that. I use some dressing to clean her up. She's got a little tear, but it's not too bad. Her white hat is red now. I leave her with the Indians and go get my car and drive it to where you are. We load her in the back seat and I take her to the hospital in Malcolm and hand her off there. And that's it. Here you are.

DE: That's it? But where was my dad in all this?

JACK: That's a question I can't answer. I was with your mom. And then you.

DE: But you must know. Did the boy ever come back? The one you sent to find him.

JACK: Curiosity killed the cat. The boy came back. Said your dad was busy. Said we was supposed to take your mom to the hospital in Malcolm.

DE: Busy with the other injuries.

JACK: Something like that.

DE: What aren't you telling me, Jack?

JACK: You are a stubborn s.o.b. I'll say this once, and only once. Your dad's doctor bag didn't have any doctoring tools in it that day. He was holding the stake.

DE: The stake?

JACK: Are you really that thick? The money. All the bets. That's what these tournaments were all about. Betting. And I heard not a few folks from town had bets on the Cubans. Your dad being one of them. Which rankled some. And he probably had a bottle or two in that bag too, along with all that money. Are you satisfied now?

I found your father with a group of men out where the cars were parked, huddled around the back of a truck. There were farmers from the district. Some of the Indians. Men from the dam and the town. They had a patch of dirt stamped flat and were throwing dice. Each man had a bunch of bills in his fist. They would throw the dice and roar and cuss and slap the bills down and count off bills and pass them around and roll the dice again. I came up to them. I had a contraction, winced in pain, then caught my breath as it passed. Lance, I said. I think I need to go. It's coming. The men stopped their activity. One of them took a pull from a mason jar of homebrew and passed it on. Lance's eyes were glassy with moonshine. He stood to his full height. For an instant, I couldn't help thinking how beautiful he still was, with his broad American shoulders and shock of black hair, his straight jaw. Even the five o'clock shadow, the gut swollen with a decade of alcoholism, the shirt smudged with dust and the tail hanging out, the broken nose — he was beautiful. I'm in the middle of something here, Ellie. Don't bother me when I'm the middle of something. A couple of the men chuckled. The baby's coming, I said. I need you. He grabbed the mason jar from someone's hand and took a drink. The hand that held the jar also held a ribbon of bills woven through his fingers. He gasped, shook his head to clear the fire from his gullet. You need to listen a little closer, he said. I'm busy. So bugger off and take that bastard with you. I stepped into the craps game and slapped his face. There was a chorus of ho-ho's from the men. Someone said, The Doc's got a feisty one.

13.

A Man Will Set Foot on the Moon

19-20 July 1969

Somewhere in the world, a clean square on a bare pine board marks the absence of a rug on a floor. Somewhere in the world a red-drenched rug marks the absence of blood in a body. Somewhere in the world a cold pale body marks the absence of a father. Once upon a time Darcy stands in front of his younger brother Dwight in the middle of the field where Dwight was born, flexing the fingers on his too-large-for-a-teenage-boy hands, man-size hands, hands already calloused and nicotine-stained, hands transforming from turtled loose fists to open-fingered butterflies, butterflies to turtles, turtles to butterflies. A dog trots to and fro between them and around them. One of the butterflies flies forth and wraps itself in a loose fist around the shiplap stick; with a deft flick Darcy tears the stick from Dwight's grasp. He cuts the air between them, once, twice, then solemnly taps Dwight first on one shoulder, then the other, as if he were a medieval duke beknighting a squire on the plain of battle. It's my stick, Dwight says. Why did you want to find me?

Darcy points the stick over his head, examines its length as if checking its plumb. He faces Dwight. Where'd you get the dog, Darcy says. Dwight shrugs. It's nobody's dog. That Amy girl's, maybe, Darcy says. He raps Dwight on the thigh, just enough to make him jump a bit. The dog bows, wags its tail, growls, barks. Follow me, Darcy says to his brother and the dog, and they do.

Behind the concession, Darcy points to patch of ground where the grass has been beaten down. Sit there, he says to Dwight. Dwight sits and settles against the wall. The plywood is warping, drawing the nails from a corner. When he looks up, he sees Darcy haloed by the porridge sky. The dog snuffles in the dirt where a small animal has excavated a hole to burrow under the shack. Darcy swings the stick and claps the earth next to the dog's snout.

I'm the man of the house now, Darcy says. Without letting go of the shiplap, he pulls a package of cigarettes from the front pocket of his pants. Buckinghams. No filter. Father's brand. One-handed, he manoeuvres a smoke into his lips and re-stows the package. From his shirt pocket, he digs out a wooden match and uses the edge of his thumbnail to spark it to life. He puffs the cigarette alight, then holds the match head down so the sliver of wood burns brightly. He tosses the lit match into the grass at Dwight's feet. A few of the stalks on a tussock catch and flame briefly before petering out. Darcy takes a drag of the cigarette, then taps Dwight on his shoe. You're gonna have to do what I tell you. You have to show your loyalty. No matter what. Dwight keeps his eyes down, scanning in the dirt to see if any hot spots are left in the blackened patch of burnt grass. He tries to pet the dog, but it skips away just beyond his reach. He drags the palm of his hand over the surface of the plywood wall, brushing off the flakes of alligatored paint. Darcy takes another deep drag of his Buckingham. He picks a piece of tobacco from his lower lip. The three of them are like subjects in a Norman Rockwell painting caught on their day off. Darcy sucking on a smoke purloined from his dead father. Dwight sunk in the dust, stripping paint from a wall. The stray dog now pissing on the corner of the building. Under a sky not blue.

Darcy squats on his haunches as easily as if settling on a stool. Does mom know you stole them smokes, Dwight says, looking up. I won't tell.

The old man don't need them now he's dead, Darcy says. I'm in charge now, Darcy says. You can't tell anybody anything. It's you and me.

Darcy flicks his cigarette into another patch of grass. He swings the scimitar-shaped shiplap, chopping the air — then cracks it across Dwight's shins. Somewhere on earth, a teenage boy rains blows on his brother, smacking the stick sharply on his legs and arms. I won't tell, Dwight says in a whisper. The dog runs to and fro and barks.

After a spell, Darcy stops hitting Dwight with the stick. He leans against the wall of the shack. A thin sheen of sweat dapples his upper lip among the suggestion of whiskers. He breathes hard through his nose and Dwight does too. Dwight lowers his arms from where they have been protecting his head. The dog stills and approaches the boys. That's a stupid dog, Darcy says. He spits at the dog, but his mouth is cotton-dry, and the small bolt of spittle falls short and rests dull in the blackened wad of burned grass. Come here, you stupid dog, Darcy says. Come on over, I got something for you. Grab that dog, Darcy says and nudges Dwight with his foot. Dwight scrambles to the dog and holds out his hand. The dog sidles over and Dwight skritches the wiry fur on its neck. The dog licks at the salt in his palm. See Spot run, Darcy says. Run, Spot, run. A slice of air, a thump, a whimper. The dog skitters away towards the bleachers, but then comes loping back near them.

Can we go home, Dwight says. He stands up and dusts off his pants.

C'mon, stupid dog, Darcy says. Come here. I got something for you. He slips a match from his shirt and holds it in the tips of his fingers. He mimes nibbling at it then holds it out. The dog ambles forward — stops — edges back — inches closer. Darcy begins to sing in a lullaby voice, matching his Jim Morrison T-shirt: *This is the end, beautiful friend, this is the end, my only friend, the end*. The dog comes over to check out Darcy's hand.

Darcy grabs the dog by the scruff of its neck and clubs it between the eyes with the stick.

Darcy, Dwight says. What'd you do that for. Darcy hits the dog again. Dwight runs at his brother and tries to tackle him but the older boy is bigger and stronger. Still keeping a grip on the stunned dog, Darcy sidesteps the lunge and uses Dwight's own momentum to drive him to the ground.

Watch this, Darcy says. He arcs the stick high over his head, brings it down in the middle of the dog's back. The sound of a large bone snapping. He lets go of the dog. See Spot run, he says. Run, Spot, run. The dog's back is broken. It struggles to its forefeet, drags itself a step, and stumbles. Blood runs from its lips. Other than laboured breathing, it doesn't make a sound.

Dwight is crying. Get up, Darcy says. When he gets to his feet, Darcy thrusts the stick at him. Your turn, Darcy says.

No, he says. He wheels but before he can get away Darcy grabs him by the back of his pants. He delivers a tap to the top of Dwight's head.

I'm in charge now, Darcy says. You have to show your loyalty.

I won't tell, Dwight says.

Take the fucking stick, Darcy says. He has Dwight by the front of his shirt now, and shakes him. The dog has managed to drag itself a few yards away, but has stopped again. It coughs. Pink bubbles froth from its nose. Dwight has the stick in his hand. Hit the stupid dog, Darcy says. Dwight closes his eyes and turns his head and flails with the stick, cutting the air. Darcy slaps his face with an open hand. Do it, he says.

Dwight shuffles to the dog. He hits the dog in the hindquarters, a glancing blow. The dog seems to grunt, but doesn't yelp. It has no feeling below the point where its spinal cord is severed. Harder, Darcy says.

I'm sorry, Dwight says. He slams the stick into the dog. I'm sorry, he says again. He lifts his arm high. As he beats the dog to death, he cries. I'm sorry. Stupid dog, he says. Stupid stupid dog. Somewhere in the world, a clean square on a bare pine board marks the absence of a rug on a floor. Somewhere, up beyond the clouds, beyond the atmosphere, across a light-second of space, three men in a spacecraft are preparing to orbit the moon. Fuck dog fucking stupid, Dwight says. He stops when his arm tires, when he pants for breath, when his tears dry. He looks at the dog. It is bleeding and broken. Yet still its rib cage rises and falls. Die, you stupid dog, Dwight says.

Do it, Darcy says. He stands, leaning slightly forward on the balls of his feet. His expression is grim, brow furrowed, like a construction foreman watching a labourer dig ditches. His hands: turtles to butterflies, butterflies to turtles, turtles to butterflies.

Dwight grips the shiplap scimitar in both hands, draws it high over his head and swings with all his might to crush the dog's skull. The dog twitches then goes still, a hide-bound bag of meat and blood and bones. Dwight leans forward and throws up in the dirt. His funeral shoes are splattered with gore and vomit. Dog's blood speckles his trousers. Darcy hasn't moved, his stare transfixed on the dog. Dwight swings the stick, still in both hands, from his crouch. He connects squarely with the side of Darcy's head. Darcy falls from the knees, going all the way down face first, raising a cloud of dust as his chest thumps the ground. He shakes himself to all fours. With one hand on the wall of the shack, he wavers to his feet.

OK, Darcy says. I won't tell. He probes at his temple. The curl of his ear is bleeding. I don't think you broke my skull, Darcy says. I got a hard fucking head. Remember that the next time you poleaxe me.

Darcy smokes a cigarette. He offers one to Dwight, who declines. They pile grass and twigs and Darcy puts the dog on top and then lights the pyre, but the flames won't catch and Darcy finally runs out of matches. They work in silence. Darcy takes off his treasured Jim Morrison T-shirt and ties up the sleeves. By the time they stuff the dog's corpse into the makeshift sack, blood has streaked Darcy's torso. They kick at the dirt to obliterate the stain on the ground. Then they retrace the route Dwight has taken earlier that day, down the service road. The same truck passes them, this time going from the town to the lower dam, and the same man tips his hat in salute. If he notices the boys are carrying a dead dog wrapped in a T-shirt he doesn't let on. They use the stick to crash through the scrub until they arrive at the cliff. They piss into the river. Darcy picks up the shrouded corpse.

One tough dog, Darcy says. He heaves the dog, and they watch as it describes its parabola through the air, cartwheeling end over end, up to the crest of its apogee then falling to the water below. The current slides it away around the bend. Won't it get stuck in the turbine, Dwight says. No, Darcy says. Dwight makes to throw the stick but Darcy stops him. Keep it, he says.

They scramble down the rocky ledge, heading upstream away from the dog. At a place at the river's edge they stop and clean up. Darcy splashes water on his torso and laves his ear. Dwight cleans his shoes. They wash their hands, using the coarse river silt to rub their hands until they are red and cold.

They crawl through the hole in the fence. They go to their house where their mother will have already gone to lie down.

Tomorrow they will attend a funeral for their father at a funeral home in Caxton. The only people there will be Dwight, Darcy and their mother. Laugh Jack will drive them in the station wagon, but he will stay outside. The boys will discover their father has been cremated. Back in Seep, all of them — Dwight, Darcy, mother and Laugh Jack — will follow the same bushwhacked trail to the cliff. Mother will take the lid from the simple white ceramic urn. Laugh Jack will doff his hat, and the mother will say, Oh for God's sake, Jack, leave the damn thing on. It will be a windy, sunny afternoon, the porridge sky having given way to the blue dome. The mother will shake the ashes from the urn and the wind will take them and flatten them and spread them into the river. Dwight will notice that some of the ashes are fine and blow a long way, while other bits are bigger and fall like pebbles. Then she will smash the urn on the rock. No one will cry. Back at the house they will eat sandwiches carved from the ham that some of the ladies have brought over. They will sit in the front room by a clean square on a bare pine-board floor. On television, they will watch a signal from up beyond the blue dome now gloaming in the dusk, where a man will set foot on the moon.

Years will pass. Dwight and Darcy will tell no one. Ever.

Lance swayed. His eyes were brimming with steady hate. If you don't get out of my sight forthwith I shall fracture your skull, he said. I could smell the sour mash emanating from him. He gathered a hawk of green phlegm and spat it on the ground between my feet. Now fuck off, you cunt cow, he said.

14.

The Wild Mouse

15 July 1999 - 10 May 2009

Ten years ago. Happy families are all alike. Fucked up families have their own fuck-upedness. Tolstoy said it more elegantly. Ten years ago. Dwight's family gathered around him, in Sara's parent's guest house. His soon-to-be-wife Sara, how soon not entirely worked out, they just knew soon, maybe later that summer ten years ago, maybe the following spring, maybe in the winter, on a Caribbean beach — her parents, the Smithsons, dropping hints about paying for a fly-in extravaganza. Her parents in the house proper a stone's throw away. His teenage daughter Julee, whom he hasn't seen in years, delivered up to him from a born-again commune by the cipher of long-estranged ex-wife Sandi-now-Esther. And Julee a cipher herself, uttering only monosyllable answers to direct questions, but her eyes like saucers as she watched everything. His brother Darcy, conjuring himself out of a wisp of crack smoke in a truck Dwight assumed was stolen or otherwise ill-gotten, now jonesing in a bedroom, the living room, the kitchen. His mother, not quite there, but an hour and a half down the road past the sweep of the road at the Waldron pasture. And his boxes of archives, almost family too, those notes, tapes, yellowing scraps in plastic protectors, photos, xeroxes, ephemera.

Later, he could see it was a bomb waiting for the right fuse.

Dwight drove as if on automatic pilot. He didn't yet know that he would never transcribe the interview with Laugh Jack. He had heard his birth story recounted so many times before, but Jack had offered new information that unsettled his understanding of the event. He had never deluded himself that his birth was like a moment from *The Lion King*, where the baboon lifts the princely child for all to cherish. But he had imagined that his arrival had been heralded by some — at least his father. But in Jack's telling, his father obviously had a more complicated role — and even as Jack hinted at the animosity between his mother and father on that day, Dwight knew there was more.

He piloted his Mazda through the rain that threatened to turn to sleet as he crested the top of the pass at Scott Lake Hill. Mid-July and almost freezing. The sky a bit clearer to the east over where the city was; the lowering grey smudge that stretched from the mountains to the top of the hill tore itself into patches like shredded and soiled kleenex. How would Julee and Sara and Dwight make out at the fair-grounds on such a day? They would not have to wait in any lineups for amusements in weather like this, but neither would they have much joy at the top of the double Ferris wheel. He looped through the Cougarspaw Road exit and then turned into Sara's parents' long drive.

Darcy's truck was gone — he had pledged that he would let Sara drive. It was the first time Darcy had left the house, had even gone out the door, since the day the week before when he had showed up spitting cherry pits. Every time Dwight and Sara and Julee had left, Dwight expected the truck and Darcy to have disappeared by the time he returned. But Darcy had stayed. He sweated the sheets for two days. Then he sat on the couch thumbing the TV remote. He had begun to eat again. He cooked omelettes at all hours. He drank buckets of juice.

Sara seemed to accept the situation with calm and grace. At night, in bed, she asked Dwight about his relationship with Darcy. It's really a mess, Dwight said.

How long has Darcy been an addict, Sara said.

Forever, Dwight said.

That's so sad, Sara said. He's so fragile.

No, he's not, Dwight said. He's a monster.

A fragile monster, Sara said. Like me.

You're not a monster, Dwight said.

We're all monsters, Sara said.

Darcy had tried to teach Julee how to play cribbage, but she refused to call out the counts of the cards, and Darcy grew bored counting her fifteens for her. Now they played silent games of crazy eights.

Dwight parked and entered the house. He put the two cassette tapes from his recorder on the kitchen table and fetched an archive box. He was affixing labels to the recordings of Laugh Jack's second interview when Mr. Smithson walked in.

Great day if it don't rain, Smithson said. He took off his battered cowboy hat and tapped it on the crisp jeans of his thigh to shed the raindrops from the felt. The shoulders of his jean jacket were splattered.

It irked Dwight that Smithson would just walk in without knocking. Yes, it was his house, his land, and Dwight and his gang were there by dint of grace and favour. But a knock, at least. That Easter, when Sara and he were visiting, Smithson had walked in and talked to them for an hour while they stayed seated on the couch, naked from the waist down, with only an afghan blanket drawn quickly over their bare parts. Sara thought it was hilarious, but Dwight kept thinking, the blanket was crocheted, with holes as big as half dollars. Well, you know what they say, Mr. Smithson. Wait twenty minutes and the weather'll change.

Yes, Mr. Eliot, that's what they say. He exaggerated the "mister." Everybody called Sara's father just by his last name, Smithson, even his wife. But not Dwight. If Smithson insisted on calling Dwight "Mr. Eliot," Dwight would insist on calling Smithson "Mr. Smithson." Smithson wiped his shiny cowboy boots on the mat by the door. He was dressed every inch the rancher, without the dirt. He was still a lawyer under the hat.

Dwight finished the labels and sealed the tapes in a Ziploc freezer bag. Have you heard from Sara and the gang, Dwight asked.

Nope, Smithson said. He pulled up a chair and turned it around so he straddled it backwards. That irked Dwight too. Smithson put the hat on his knee. Then he continued: But a couple of gentlemen dropped by asking about your brother.

Dwight took the freezer bag and rifled through the folders in the archive box until he found the one from last week: Laugh Jack Interview. He used a Sharpie to add an "s" to "Interview" and slid today's tapes in. The possibilities of who the gentlemen were seemed too profuse to imagine. Detectives. Bikers. Drug dealers. Finally, Dwight merely said, And?

They weren't looking for your brother, exactly. Smithson undid the pearl snap on his shirt pocket and withdrew a business card. They were looking for that truck of his. Smithson slid the card across the table. XL Recovery and Restitution, the card said. Experts in Asset Recovery. There was a name written in pen on the card: Mr. White, and a phone number with a 604 area code. His colleague was Mr. Black, Smithson said.

Dwight exhaled a deep breath. I can't really answer for Darcy, he said. It's his business.

These men come to my house, Smithson said. It's my business.

Dwight let that one hang.

What do you know about Sara, Smithson said.

Pardon, Dwight said.

Let me put it this way, Mr. Eliot. Men like your brother are not a novelty to my daughter. Dwight thought he maintained a blank expression, but something in the way he adjusted his posture, settling into the chair, or the way he began to flick the edge of the repo man's card sent a clue to the older man. I gather she's never mentioned her checkered past to you, Smithson said.

No, Dwight said. The two men sat at the table. Smithson sat very still, one hand on the chair back, the other on his hat. His gaze never left Dwight. Dwight stopped fidgeting with the business card, drummed his fingers on the table, enumerated the appliances on the counter: toaster, microwave, blender, can opener, coffee maker. He watched a fly beat lazily against the window over the sink. He met Smithson's gaze. They sat for what seemed a long time for the situation — thirty seconds, a minute, two minutes. Dwight's father had always said about negotiation: the first one to open his mouth loses. Smithson was a good negotiator. Finally Dwight said, She told me she was like a hippie. Free spirit.

Mr. Eliot, Sara has been through some dire experiences. She has come very far and that was a long time ago. But dragons have a way of reawakening, as I'm sure you know. Let me repeat, men like your brother are not a novelty.

Dwight stood up. Then sat down again. Jesus, he said. Fuck.

I have made inquiries, Mr. Eliot. I do not believe, despite your own tendencies to test the outcomes of games of chance, that you are an immoral man. But I cannot say the same for your brother.

Inquiries? said Dwight. I quit gambling years ago.

I am a man of not inconsiderable means. And I do not sit idly by to watch loved ones undone by the venalities of those who may do them harm. Smithson stood up. You will solve this, Mr. Eliot. You will go into town and find Sara and your brother and your daughter. You are welcome to come back here. We will talk further. We will be frank about how we will succeed. Smithson moved to the door. But your brother is not welcome. And if he presents himself on my property, I will use my not inconsiderable means to make him more miserable than he already is.

Dwight stood up. OK, he said.

Sara has my cellular phone. You call her and find her and get her, Smithson said.

Yes, Dwight said.

Smithson walked to the door. I let those gentlemen know they took

143

that truck to the Stampede, Smithson said. So they all might need a ride by the end of the day. Home, or wherever. Smithson donned his hat. Men like that, Mr. White and Mr. Black, they're pretty good at finding what they're looking for.

Smithson left.

Dwight went to the window. Mrs. Smithson — Molly, Dwight had no problem calling her Molly — was standing in the driveway with an umbrella. She met her husband and they linked arms and walked to the big house. Dwight cupped his hand over the fly, inert now, then lifted it. The fly hesitated, then buzzed up to the ceiling and through the archway into the living room.

Dwight dialled Sara. It rang and rang then went to voice mail. He left a message and dialled again. The fifth time he called, she answered. Hullo, Sara said.

Dwight could hear music in the background, loud country music. Sara, Dwight said. It's me. Where are you?

Hey Dwight! We're just taking a break out of the rain. Her voice was loud. Just shouting over the din? Dwight thought he detected a hint of intoxication. He and Sara didn't drink much — Dwight didn't have much interest in alcohol. But he had seen her occasionally get drunk with friends. It was two in the afternoon. He didn't ask her.

Where's Julee? Dwight said.

She's right here! Sara said. Where else would she be?

Where are you?

The sound of the band chanting the chorus to "Cadillac Ranch" — Cadillac, Cadillac — marked the hesitation before she answered. Dusty's Saloon, Sara said. We're having fun, Dwight. Darcy even taught Julee how to two-step.

She's not legal age, Dwight said. You have to leave. I'm on my way. Meet me at the midway. By the clock. He was already wearing his rain slicker, holding the keys to the Mazda in his hand.

What? Sara said.

144

Leave. Get Julee out of there. I'll meet you —

We have to wait for Darcy, Sara said. He'll never find us if we leave now.

Where is he? Dwight said.

He went out with some friends he met. He knows everyone. He said he'd be back right away. I've got to wait for him, Sara said. Julee! Julee! It's your dad. Do you want to talk to your dad? The noise from the phone ricocheted in his ear as it sounded like it was being passed around. Then Sara's voice again: She gave you a little wave. She doesn't want to talk. She's not much of a talker is she Darcy?

Is Darcy there?

No, I told you he went out for a bit.

You said "she doesn't talk much, Darcy." You called me "Darcy." Is he there? Don't let him go, Dwight said.

I didn't say "Darcy" I said "Dwight." It's hard to hear here. Hey, that's mine. Don't touch that, Sara said.

What?

Sorry, honey, some asshole was trying to steal my drink. Cowboys! Sara said.

Sara, listen to me, Dwight said. On the other end, the song ended and cheers rose. Unintelligible stage banter. Sara. Are you there.

Of course I am, where else would I be.

Is Julee drinking? Tell me she's not drinking, Dwight said.

Of course she is silly, Sara said.

Sara. Sara. Get out of —

Tomato juice! You have tomato juice don't you sweetie? Sara said.

Sara. You've got to go. Some men are looking for Darcy, they came to your dad's house.

Darcy went with some friends, I told you that. He's coming back with a surprise.

Sara. Leave that place. Forget about Darcy. You never want to see him ever again. There are men looking for Darcy. They are going to repossess his truck. Do you understand? He is about to relapse if he hasn't already, Dwight said. You can't be around him. Julee can't be there.

What? Sara said.

You have to go now, Dwight said. There are men who are looking for Darcy. They want his truck. Do you hear me? There are men who are coming to repossess his truck.

No, he didn't take his truck, Sara said. He left with his friends. Someone's going to steal his truck?

Not steal it, Darcy said. They're repo men. Repossess. Fuck. I'll phone you when I get into town.

I'm not leaving until he gets back, Sara said.

Sara.

It's too noisy, honey. And the battery's beeping. Hey, I gotta go. He heard her give a shriek of laughter as the phone cut off and he imagined some beefy oil executive in a pink shirt and Tony Lama boots yanking her by the arm to the dance floor.

He drove the Mazda to its limits, passing cars on the shoulder, running yellow lights and even a red when he got inside the city limits. The rain had slowed to a drizzle, still steady but not slick. He weaved through the rush hour traffic, then the traffic around the Stampede grounds, and pulled up to Dusty's. He double-parked in a taxi zone and hit the flashers. A doorman with the sleeves of his cowboy shirt ripped off to expose anvil-sized biceps intercepted him at the curb.

Amigo, the doorman said. You gotta move your wheels.

I'll just be a minute. I have to get my fiancée and daughter out of there, Dwight said. It'll just take a minute.

Amigo, the doorman said. See that? He gestured to a throng of people huddled under an awning that stretched down the sidewalk. The line starts there. It's an hour wait. Unless you got a VIP pass. Move your car.

No, I'm not staying. They're in trouble.

What kind of trouble? the doorman said.

My fiancée's been drinking. Dwight said.

Mister, there's a lot of fiancées in there right now drinking. What makes yours so special.

She's an alcoholic, I think, Dwight said.

The doorman smirked. I think there's a few alcoholic fiancées in there too, Buddy. Move your car, get in line, and pay the cover like everyone else.

My daughter's underage, Dwight said.

The doorman hesitated, then turned away. He hit a button on his belt and spoke into his headset. He turned back to Dwight. OK. It's like this. You give me the keys to your car, and your wallet, the doorman said. Dwight did. The doorman gripped his arm and continued: If you're not back here in five fucking minutes I'm gonna slash the tires on this piece of shit and put it on the hook. He nodded to a tow truck that was idling up the street. And then I'm gonna come inside, find you, and hurt you. Capeesh? I'll lay a fucking hurt on you. He squeezed Dwight's arm like he was juicing a pomegranate, then shoved him to the entryway where another doorman, bigger than the first, had appeared to usher him along. Some of those waiting in line hollered a protest. Shut the fuck up, you monkeys, the first doorman called. Man's gotta rescue a virgin. Catcalls.

Dwight hadn't been inside Dusty's for years — maybe twenty years. But like any male who had been raised within one hundred miles of Calgary, and had been to the Calgary Stampede between the ages of fifteen and thirty, he had been there before. It hadn't changed. The men were in uniform — jeans, hats, boots. Oil Patch office workers — geologists, engineers, IT guys, accountants, sales reps — duded themselves up in creased Wranglers and two-toned Nashville shirts, hats as wide as their shoulders, exotic-skinned boots. They mingled with real cowboys from the rodeo, whose hats were a little more beaten, whose shirts sported sponsor logos, whose jeans were muddied, and whose boots were as likely to be lace-up ropers as they were typical shitkickers. The women tended to costume themselves with more variety — some of the office crowd in mannish jeans and hats, some in long denim dresses; but there were women in little black dresses and heels, halter tops and Daisy Duke cut-offs (despite the weather), t-shirts and mini-skirts. It smelled like beer and body odour and mildewing fireproofed straw bales, mingled but unmasked by wafts of perfume and deodorant as cleavaged waitresses moved through the crowd with trays of drinks hoisted in the air. Smoking was still allowed in bars then, and the lights in their fixtures warmed the nicotine residue laid down over the decades, and added to the smoke of the Export As and Player's unfiltereds and Camels and Old Port cigars circulating in the room, to deposit a bitter taste of tobacco on the back of the tongue. Straw and peanut shells crunched underfoot. Dwight jostled through the shoulder-tight crowd, dodging but not always missing elbows and heels, moving from table to table as he scanned the barn-like room for Sara, Julee, and Darcy. The band cycled through its playlist — they played with an edge, electrified Hank Williams Sr., Steve Earle, Stevie Ray. The rhythm guitarist broke out a fiddle and they ripped into Charlie Daniels. Dwight was vaguely aware that he had been more than five minutes as he tried to canvass the servers to see if they remembered the trio he was looking for. Most gave him a blank stare or a quick brush-off, as if to say, How do you expect me to keep track of five hundred drunks? But then one said, Yeah, I saw them. They left. Then she turned to serve chilled vodka shots to a tableful of oil company landmen.

A hand gripped his arm — a bouncer. He allowed himself to be led towards the door, but they stopped near the bar where they were joined by another man. The manager. The three of them — Dwight and the Dusty's staff — had a short conversation with the barman. They had to yell to be heard, and spoke in short cut-off cadences.

No luck, the manager said. He didn't look at Dwight when he spoke. His eyes ceaselessly scanned the throng.

A waitress thought she saw them, Dwight yelled.

What'd they look like, the bouncer yelled.

A guy. Big. Jean jacket. Ponytail. Rough-looking. My fiancée: blonde, kinda small. Really short hair. Daughter — young. Long straight brown hair. Kind of peasant dress.

I saw 'em, the bartender yelled. Guy downing J.D. doubles. Woman, vodka tonics. Girl, tomato juice. Weird bunch.

The bouncer turned and nodded. He remembered them.

The manager yelled. They left. They're gone.

How do you know? Dwight yelled. He thought he detected eye contact between the bouncer and the manager. The barman turned away and was pouring orders again.

They were moving, the bouncer expertly guiding Dwight to the door and out onto the sidewalk. The manager melted into the room. As Dwight moved away from the building some of the crowd behind the rope let out a cheer, and someone called, Where's your old lady, buddy. Scattered laughter. The inside bouncer passed Dwight over to the bare-arm doorman, who escorted him to his car. Tough luck, amigo, the doorman said. Maybe they went to Outlaw's or something.

Dwight drove a couple of blocks up to the Co-op gas station on Macleod Trail. The clerk wouldn't give him change for the payphone unless he purchased something. He bought a Kit Kat bar with a twenty, scooped the quarters and dimes into his hand. He waited while a young woman whose low-ride jeans exposed at least half her buttocks yelled into the receiver. She was carrying a giant and soaking stuffed dog and every few seconds tried to hitch her pants up without letting go of the dog. She slammed down the phone. What the fuck are you looking at you fucking pervert, she said to Dwight. Her mascara ran from where she had been crying. Fuck off, she said. Dwight slotted coins into the phone and punched the number for the cellphone Sara had. It rang and rang then went through to voice mail. He thought about phoning Smithson, but didn't. He tried the cellphone again. Voice mail. Dead battery?

He went to the car. The young woman sat on the curb next to it, hugging her dog. You OK, Dwight said.

Yeah, the woman said. Then: No, she said. She punched the dog. Bastard, she said. Then she looked at Dwight. You OK, she said.

No, Dwight said.

Fucking Calgary fucking Stam-fucking-pede, the woman said. Can you give me a ride, she said.

No, Dwight said. I gotta find some people.

Yeah, me too, the woman said. I need to go home. Dwight gave her twenty dollars for a cab then got in his car. He drove the few blocks up Macleod Trail and pulled into the big parking lot across from the Stampede grounds. On a sunny day there would have been no spots by this time of day, but with the cold and rain the attendant with the orange vest waved him in. Another twenty dollars out of his wallet. He drove up and down the rows and wasn't surprised when he saw a big Dodge Ram 4x4 that looked like Darcy's wheels. He found a spot two cars over and went to look in the truck. The box with cherries still behind the seats. The rings burned in the fabric roof inside the cab. He went to his car and scrawled a note to stick under the wiper — Call Smithson. Do not leave till you find me. My car is down the row. — Dwight.

Dwight mounted the steps of the pedestrian overpass that led from the parking lot over Macleod to the fairgrounds. The rain had ceased. He stopped at another payphone and tried the cell, then phoned Smithson. Molly answered.

Hi, it's Dwight, he said. He used as light a tone as he could muster in his voice.

Hello, Dwight, Molly said. I'll get Smithson.

No, no, Dwight said. You can just pass along a message.

I'll get him, Molly said. A shuffle and clunk on the line indicated the phone had been put down on the kitchen counter. Then another line clicked open. No greeting, just: Smithson.

Dwight waited for the click that would tell him Molly had hung up her phone, but it never came. The he said: Hi, Mr. Smithson. I'm just calling —

Did you find them, Smithson said.

No, no, not yet, Dwight said. I'm just heading to the grounds to meet up with them.

Have you talked to them, Smithson said.

Not exactly, no, Dwight said. I just left a note on the truck —

You found the truck, Smithson said.

— I just wanted to check to see if they had called you or left a message, Dwight said. The cellphone battery must —

Mr. White and Mr. Black will also find it, Smithson said.

Mr. Smithson, Dwight said. I will find them. I know they're here. I left a note for them to call you.

Hmmph, Smithson said.

Tell them to wait for me. I'll keep checking the clock tower. Tell them to wait for me at the clock tower.

You will bring my daughter home, Mr. Eliot.

Yes, I will, said Dwight. And mine too.

But not your brother, Smithson said.

No, not him.

Good day, Smithson said.

Smithson's phone went dead, but the line stayed open. Molly. Molly. Are you still there, Dwight said. Tell them to meet me at the clock tower, Molly. Now the connection ended, replaced by a dial tone.

Dwight entered the vast fairground. Over the nearly ninety years that the Stampede had been going on, the Stampede Board had expanded its land base to swallow up hundreds of acres of what had once been neighbourhoods and businesses. In the southeast corner, hard by the slow flow of the Elbow River, where it bent towards its mouth at the Bow

River, stretched the rodeo grounds and the barns and stables to support the bronco busting, bull riding, calf roping, barrel racing, steer wrestling, and the nightly extravaganza of chuckwagon racing. The Indian Village was sandwiched between the rodeo grandstand and the river at the far southern end, its entrance marked by the world's largest wooden flagpole. The agriculture buildings and the show rings, where the heavy horses, cutting horses, the ox-pulls, the 4-H Club competitions paraded throughout the day, accumulated to the east, between the chuckwagon oval and the midway. The exhibition buildings and arena — The Big Four Building, the Round-up Centre, The Corral, Saddledome, with their hawkers selling slicers and dicers and Swiffers and mops, quilting presentations, SuperDog shows, sheepdog trials, and grand casino — swept along the western edge and curved to contain the property on the north. In the centre, running more or less north to south, the midway unfolded in all its glory — the Ferris wheels single and double, the bungee slingshot, the Zipper, the Wild Mouse, all the rides, games of chance, corn dog and root beer stands, basketball and ring toss games, guess-your-weight and temporary tattoo concessions, outdoor stages, indoor beer gardens, sweepstakes booths sponsored by community organizations — the dream house, win-a-car-a-day, the gold brick.

The inclement weather meant attendance was down for the day, but Dwight knew there would still be tens of thousands of fairgoers. Just six days ago, on the day after Julee and Sara flew in and Darcy showed up on his doorstep, he and Julee and Sara had visited the Stampede after watching the parade (Darcy had stayed home, detoxing). Smithson had treated them all to his corporate box seats next to the judging platform for the parade, and then premium infield seats for the rodeo. That day the temperature had climbed to thirty degrees Celsius, and the one hundred thousand people at the grounds had shared sunburns. Today, the midway seemed merely busy with rain-slickered families and umbrella-toting couples. Dwight took a moment to come up with a search strategy. He figured Darcy would gravitate to the beer gardens and the casino. But he knew his brother had also been an aficionado of the mid-way rides — riding the Zipper once for ten consecutive times on a bet. Sara — the Sara he knew — would be interested in the craft displays, the Ag barns, the heavy horse-pulls. But she could be tempted to go on the rides. Julee. His daughter had been here a week, and they hadn't had a real conversation. She just stared. She had been very upset last Friday at the rodeo, and hid her face in her hands to avoid watching the steer wrestling and the cowboys fall on their heads when the bulls bucked them off. And the chuckwagons had been hell — two wagons touched wheels on the backstretch and one of the teams went down in a heap of horses and wagon and men. One of the animals began to thrash and neigh with a sound like a wounded soldier. They brought the track's horse ambulance out, set up a shroud, and euthanized two of the horses as they lay in their traces. Julee wouldn't be anywhere near the rodeo.

He started walking. He walked and he walked and walked. The smell of cinnamon and dough cooked in fat wafted from the mini-donut fryers. Children gnawed at corn dogs and Fiddlestix. Rock music blared from the Matterhorn ride — *Do you want to go faster?* the ride jockeys hollered through the speakers from their operators' booths. Bells rang. Screams of delight and the whoosh of compressed air erupted from the Drop of Doom. A witch cackled from a funhouse. Two young girls staggered out of the Starship 3000, one of them stopping to puke in a trash can. Flappers clicked through the pins on the Over/Under and Crown & Anchor game wheels. Rubber hammers whacked rubber moles. A child cried. Carnies barked. Electrical generators throbbed, hydraulics whirred and hissed, traction chains caught on coaster cars. Dwight stopped at a Ring-the-Bell joint to ask the carny if he had seen Darcy. This was the kind of thing that would appeal to Darcy. Show off his strength. To Dwight's surprise, the carny said, Sure, they been here. Really, Dwight said. How long ago.

I dunno, an hour, two hours ago. A while. Like you said, biker-looking dude. Two chicks, one old one young. Dropped enough scratch that he walked away with choice for each of the ladies.

What did they choose, Dwight said.

A big fucking plush, man, the carny said. What the fuck else are they gonna choose. Are you gonna play or what?

Dwight went on. Now he knew what he was looking for: Julee, Sara, Darcy, and two big fucking plushes. He entered the casino. Julee was underage for the casino, but Darcy had snuck her into Dusty's. Or else Darcy and Sara would park Julee somewhere and come to play. It was busier inside, as the crowds sought respite from the cold. Dwight wandered from table to table. At the craps table he hesitated and reached his hand into his pocket to touch the few bills. The red Lucite dice bounced and came to rest. A shout rose from the gamblers; the thrower made his point. The universe seemed to shrink to a twelve-foot by five-foot plane of green felt, with all its possible permutations reduced to those determinable between the numbers two and thirty-six. It would be so easy to lay a twenty on the pass line, forty more once the point was made, and play one round. Four years since his last bet. He had his hand out of his pocket, money ready. Then he pivoted on his heel and made his way past the blackjack pits, the roulette game, the crazy sic bo with its myriad bets. Near the door a ganglion of gamblers cheered or groaned as players took turns tossing coins in the air using a wooden paddle with a handle. A poster board advertised the game as two-up, from Australia. Wagers were with real money, not chips — a loonie or toonie at a time. From the makeup of the crowd and the odds posted, Dwight surmised it was a rube's game. He jingled some of the change in his pocket, but moved on. He checked the bar upstairs from the casino, where hatted men drank Bud Light and gnawed at steak sandwiches while they kept an eye on the keno board. But no Julee, Sara, or Darcy.

He walked the grounds. He bought a piece of bannock in the Indian Village, then made his way among the teepees, looking in the lodges that had their flaps open to the public. There were always folks from the reserve near Seep who set up — perhaps Darcy had come here for old time's sake. Dwight nodded to a couple of people whose faces he recognized or thought he recognized, and asked around. But no one had seen them.

As he made his circuits around the exhibition, he looped back to the clock tower again and again. Several times he stopped at pay phones to call the cellphone and Smithson. The cell rang still to voice mail. Smithson took to one-word conversations:

Smithson, he answered.

It's Dwight. Any news.

Nope. Then a hang up.

Dwight sat through a sheepdog trial at the Saddledome, watched a heavy horse-pull, stood near the door while the SuperDogs jumped through hoops at the Corral. He passed by prize-winning quilts and jams, oil paintings of cattle by retirees, pitch-men and women hawking gadgets at the Round-up Centre. The sky had lightened as the day wore into evening, with patches of blue showing through rents in the clouds. Boys with squeegees pushed big puddles of standing water on the tarmac of the midway towards open storm drains. The crowds picked up.

He phoned Smithson again. This time Molly answered.

He's gone into town, Molly said. He couldn't stand sitting out here and waiting.

OK, Dwight said.

He was working his way up and down between the stalls in the Ag. Barn when he finally came upon Julee. She was standing in the aisle, among the cotton-candy-drunk toddlers and their mothers, the 4-H'ers leading washed and combed steers, the red-vested black-hatted Stampede personnel and volunteers with clipboards and walkie-talkies parting to pass her on one side or the other. Julee was watching a pair of miniature donkeys as they ate. Her long straight hair was caught up in the collar of her jacket, tangled from a day of rain and weather. She had a flat-crowned black cowboy hat dangling from strings tied around her neck — a Stampede special. When Dwight came up she turned her pale oval face to him. Her very pale grey eyes registered recognition, and her brows lifted almost imperceptibly. With both arms she was embracing a crimson plush dog, like the one the young woman at the pay phone had had, that seemed almost half her size.

Hi Julee, Dwight said. He gave her an awkward hug. The big red dog was between them.

Hi Dwight, Julee said.

You can call me Dad, Dwight said.

I know, Julee said. But I think I'll call you Dwight. She turned and looked at the donkeys. The donkeys shifted in their stall. One swung to look at Julee looking at her. The other settled into a bed of straw. They were silvery-tawny, and their coats shone from the grooming and care they received. Each had a dark dorsal stripe.

They're beautiful, aren't they, Dwight said.

I guess so, Julee said.

Julee. Where are Sara and Darcy, Dwight said. She watched the donkeys. A young woman Julee's age walked behind Dwight and Julee, leading a coal-black steer. It mooed. Julee, Dwight said.

They went away, Julee said.

Where, Dwight said. Where did they go. Are they coming back.

They just — Julee said. They just left. They said you would come for me. And you did.

How long have you been here, Dwight asked. He cupped her arm to try to move her out of the flow of people and animals. A farm boy led an Appaloosa by its bridle, coming between them and the donkeys. The break in the visual field seemed to loosen Julee from her trance. Dwight moved them to a corner of the barn. A few bales of straw offered a kind of bench and they sat down.

How long have you been here, Dwight asked again.

Oh, not long, Julee said.

Where were you before this, Dwight asked.

I was over there — Julee tossed her head in an indeterminate direction. The man trimmed the toenails on a big horse, she said.

Here in the barn, Dwight said.

Yes, Julee said. And I went on the Wild Mouse. Would you like to go on the Wild Mouse with me?

Where are Sara and Darcy, Dwight said.

I went on the Wild Mouse eight times. I have a bracelet. I can ride the Wild Mouse as often as I want. I got cold and came here, Julee said. They left. They said to go to the big clock and you would be there. So every time the Wild Mouse ended I went to the big clock.

Do you know where the cellphone is, Dwight said. Sara had a cellphone.

But you weren't there every time, Julee said. I got cold. And wet.

The cellphone, Dwight said.

Julee let one hand go from the red dog and fished in her jacket. She handed the clamshell Motorola to him. He flipped it open. The LED's flashed: 14 MISSED CALLS.

Julee, Julee, Julee, Dwight said. I've been trying to call you. Why didn't you answer.

Julee shrugged. I didn't know how, she said.

They left the Ag. Barn. Julee allowed him to hold her by the hand. She hung on tight. As they walked, Dwight used the cell and punched in Smithson's number with his thumb. Molly, he said, when she answered. I found Julee.

There was silence at the other end. Finally Molly spoke: Sara's not coming home tonight, she said.

What, Dwight said. You talked to her.

She did call, yes, Molly said. She said she was staying with friends tonight. Dwight could hear the hurt in her voice. Maybe a couple of nights. She said she needs some space.

Does Mr. Smithson know this, Dwight said. He and Julee had stopped along the avenue of fast food joints that marked the north end of the midway. He had to let go of her hand to put his finger in his ear to hear properly.

Yes, Molly said.

What did he say, Dwight asked. Can I talk to him.

Mr. Eliot, Molly said. I'm not sure you should come back here tonight. Smithson is on his way home. There was another long pause. A roar erupted somewhere to his left. Motorcycles had begun their show in the Motordrome.

Molly, Dwight said.

I think I have to go now, Molly said, and she cut the connection.

Julee had drifted a few feet away to watch the mini-donuts pop out of the fryer and into the stainless hopper, where the concessionaires slid them with paddles into little bags. Dwight said, Have you eaten anything today.

I like mini-donuts, Julee said. Dwight bought a bag of donuts, and a piece of vegetarian pizza for Julee (she didn't eat meat), and two bottles of water. By the time they left the grounds and walked up the ramp to cross to the Macleod Trail, the sky was finally beginning to darken after this long summer's day that had felt like winter. At the top of the pedestrian overpass Dwight realized that a plume of smoke emanating from the parking lot contributed to the darkening. A green Dodge Ram 4x4 was engulfed in a well-involved fire. Firefighters were using extinguishers on it, while some others were connecting a hose to a nearby hydrant. Dwight grabbed Julee's hand and ran.

They watched the fire. Dwight imagined he could smell burning cherries. What looked like the form of a man slumped behind the wheel. The firefighters ran into the thick of the blaze and forced the door open. A huge plush dog, burning fiercely, tumbled onto the ground.

The note Dwight had left on the truck was under the wiper of the Mazda. Darcy had scrawled on its reverse: Little Buddy — I have Managed to escape the Island. Signed, The Skipper. p.s. I took Ginger. Or maybe she's MaryAnn 2 you. Say hi to Mr. Howell.

He drove to Smithson's. He knew he couldn't stay there. But he couldn't leave his belongings behind. Julee sat in the passenger seat, nibbling at her mini-donuts like a squirrel. That was Uncle Darcy's truck, Dwight said. It started to rain again.

I thought so, Julee said. It was a pretty fire.

At Smithson's he drove directly to the guest house. He coaxed Julee to gather her clothes and things from her room. He moved his archive boxes three at a time into the hatchback of the Mazda, six in all, two trips. He went back into the house and started throwing his clothes into a duffel. His tape recorder. Two more trips and he had everything, at least what he would need for a few days, maybe what he would need for longer. Anything left behind was dispensable. He found Julee sitting on the edge of the bed. Her old-timey cardboard suitcase was open beside her, and a few things were in it. But she was reading a Bible. Dwight rifled through the drawers and laundry hamper, making sure nothing was overlooked. He fetched her toiletry bag from the adjoining bathroom.

Did you see my new boots, Julee suddenly said. She stretched so her legs stuck out from beneath the hem of her long dress. A brand new pair of cowboy boots, brown with roses stitched up the side in a contrasting umber. Uncle Darcy said I needed new boots. To go with my hat.

Did you keep your old shoes, Dwight said.

Julee nodded and put a hand to her slouch bag thrown over her shoulder. Dwight pressed the suitcase closed. In the driveway, Smithson and Molly waited by his car. Molly had the umbrella opened. Dwight managed to cram the suitcase in and close the hatchback. Get in the car, Julee, he said.

OK, Julee said.

Dwight walked over to Smithson. I don't know what to say, Dwight said.

No, I guess you don't. You've got nothing to say, said Smithson. There's nothing you can say.

I didn't know anything, Dwight said. About Sara.

No, I guess you didn't. The rain drummed faintly on Smithson's hat.

I'm sorry, Dwight said.

I guess you are, Smithson said. He took his hat off. Molly, he said. Hold this a minute. He handed his hat to his wife. Mr. Eliot, Smithson said, I do not doubt that your intentions were noble. But we both know what road good intentions pave.

Dwight stood in the rain.

What I'm about to do isn't exactly fair, Smithson said. But something has got to be done. He moved closer to Dwight so he stood directly in front of him, then looked him in the eye. Smithson was just a bit taller. He put his hands on the wet shoulders of Dwight's slicker, then deftly moved them up to cup the nape of his neck. With one quick motion he brought Dwight's head forward while at the same time he deftly shifted his body weight and lowered his own head slightly. The crown of his forehead met the bridge of Dwight's nose squarely with a sound like two pieces of lumber clapped together. He pulled his hands back. Dwight dropped to his knees, then reached for the ground with his hands. Blood poured from his mouth and nose. He blinked back the stars behind his eyes.

Molly handed Smithson a clean cowboy kerchief, folded and starched in a neat square. Dwight rocked out of his position on all fours and sat heavily so his ass was in the mud and his back against his car. Smithson tossed the handkerchief into his lap. Consider the wedding off, Smithson said. Goodbye, Mr. Eliot. He gathered his hat from Molly and they went to their house.

Dwight drove back to the city. The first two motels where he stopped refused him a room. The third one barely registered his quickening eyes growing ever blacker—and the broken nose, the blood soaking his face and jacket and shirt. The next few days, few weeks blurred by.

He took Julee to the fairgrounds one last time, covering his bruised face with sunglasses. The weather had turned again to summer. They rode the Wild Mouse again and again and again.

While they waited in line, Julee said, Mr. Smithson doesn't like you any more.

No, Julee, Dwight said. He doesn't.

Sara went away and now he doesn't like you, she said.

Yes, Dwight said.

So he smashed your face, Julee said. With his head.

They rode the Wild Mouse.

He had no way of phoning Julee's mom, his ex-wife, Sandi-now-Esther, so he flew back with Julee himself, maxing out his credit card for the ticket. Julee insisted on carrying her big red dog onto the plane as carry-on. At the Hamilton airport, Sandi-now-Esther glanced at him once, registered the eyes and nose, then didn't look at him again. Mother and daughter walked hand in hand to the baggage carousel, talking and laughing. I've never heard Julee laugh, Dwight thought, as he lagged a few paces behind. Not even on the Wild Mouse. When Julee picked up her suitcase Dwight stepped forward, and gently touched her arm. Julee, he said.

She turned. Thank you very much, Dwight, she said. The Stampede was fun. She put down her suitcase and shook his hand. She held the big red dog in her other arm. Sandi-now-Esther paid no attention, as if he were invisible.

He came back to Calgary. He found a cheap apartment, moved his archives into a closet. He declined to re-register in his Library Sciences graduate program back east, abandoned his thesis project. Every day he touched his nose. The eyes went from black to blue to eggplant to yellow. He drove by casinos in the dark of night but never went in. He took a job in the corporate archives of International Horizon Corp, formerly International Hydrocarbons, formerly Industrial Heat & Coal, originally Prairie Mountain Light & Power. He saved some money, until he had the down payment on a house. He got promoted. Twice a month he drove up and down Highway 22 to visit his mother, along the sweep of road around the Waldron. When Laugh Jack died, he asked her if she wanted to go the funeral, She said no. He didn't go either. Ten years passed. Until one day, he met his house coming down the road.

That slap was the last time I remember touching your father. You were born in the middle of the riot. Jack attended. You know all that. We continued to live in Seep. I put a lock on the bedroom door, not that I needed it. When your father was home he slept on the floor or on the couch or on the rug.

15.

The Crux of the Biscuit

8-23 July 2009

Just as the giant birds of prey, like Golden Eagles, when they set out on solitary migrations across the continent, passing as they do every spring and summer through the skies over Seep, abandon the familiar routines of hunting, social communion, and the diurnal routines of action and rest, and instead apply themselves to their near ceaseless labours of flight in a singular pursuit of their goal, so too Dwight abandoned his nightly trips to casinos and poker rooms in order to apply himself to the website for the Coalition for Assured Responsible Development. He added a page to the WordPress blog that served as the CARD website to describe the annual raptor migration, how the birds as they passed over, looked down on the site with their keen eyesight and despaired at what they witnessed.

Not that he gave up gambling entirely — for every two hours he worked on the website, he allowed himself an hour of online Texas Hold'em. He moved his mouse over the bookmarks bar where he had placed a shortcut to his favourite Cayman Island-based gaming engine and won or lost a few hundred dollars. Most nights, he could hear Darcy riffing his way through classic-rock chord progressions on the Telecaster at the same time he watched marathon sessions of *Intervention* and *Celebrity Rehab with Dr. Drew* on the television in the basement. As the night progressed, with the taste of each no-name beer Darcy drank by the dozen, the snippets of songs became increasingly truncated and ragged, and the yelling at the television more frequent. Then the music would stop. Some nights the snoring began. Other nights Darcy would come upstairs and loom in the doorway to the home office.

Darcy sniffed the air. Fuck you, Dwight, Darcy said. It smells like the kill floor at the Cargill plant.

Dwight sniffed an armpit. He had the window to the office wide open, and an oscillating fan attempted to cool the room down. But the heat of the day still hung in the house. Smells like a rose to me, Dwight said.

That was the worst job I ever fucking had, Darcy said. He moved into the room and took a seat in the worn-out La-Z-Boy tucked in a corner. Lay waste to two thousand, maybe twenty-five hundred head every twelve-hour shift. Darcy stuck his feet out, crossed his legs at the ankles. Every ten or fifteen seconds, a beef in the box, aim the captive bolt gun — *pow!* — in the brains.

I'm trying to get some work done here, Dwight said.

You eat meat, Darcy said. If you eat meat, you gotta hear this story.

I don't think so, Dwight said.

You got that slaughterhouse smell goin' for you, Darcy said. Fact is, only reason I got a job at a fucking slaughterhouse was because you fired my ass. Or did you forget that part.

You were caught snorting coke, Dwight said. By my boss. What was I supposed to do.

Details, Darcy said. Minor details.

And you tried to set fire to the ATCO trailer I was in.

Don't remember that part, Darcy said. You wouldn't open the door and face me like a man. Like a brother. The crux of the biscuit is the apostrophe, like Frank says.

Frank, Dwight said.

Zappa, Darcy said. Frank fucking Zappa. Darcy made an electric guitar buzzing noise with his lips and strummed air guitar on his gut.

I'm busy, Dwight said. Go away.

Ended up on the kill floor. The iron blanket of death covered us, Darcy said. This old Mexican dude that worked there, that's what he called it. "The iron blanket of death." Iron, on the account of the blood. He was a sticker. Darcy mimed plunging a knife into the neck of a cow. Dwight fiddled with his computer. Fresh death. Darcy shut his eyes and tilted his head back. He found the gearshift for the chair and yanked, lifting his legs into the air. The month I worked there, I'd come back to where I was crashing and I'd be sore and stiff everywhere. My hands were like hamburger. Ha ha. I had blisters on my feet. The blood worked into your boots. Every time I brained a beef I'd clench my balls. Two thousand times a shift, clench my balls. I swear to god, even my nut muscles were stiff. Darcy, he said, addressing himself, you will burn in hell.

Your cremaster, Dwight said.

Huh, Darcy said. He opened his eyes to look at his brother.

The muscle structure that contracts your testicles, Dwight said. It's called your cremaster. It's what regulates —

Don't be such a fucking milk-brained stooge, Darcy said. I'm telling you a fucking story. When I killed a beef, I got stiff balls. Capeesh?

They're involuntary muscles, Dwight said. They don't actually strain, I don't think. You probably had a hernia.

Darcy put one hand down near his groin, palm outward at a right angle to his body, and cupped his other hand around his ear. Whazzat, he said. He paused a moment, as if carrying on a phone conversation. Izzat right, he said. OK, I'll let him know. He put his hands on the armrests. I just got a call from my creamsicles, Darcy said. They said to tell you, you don't know jack shit. That's the crux of the biscuit.

Are you going to let me work, Dwight said.

Be my guest, Darcy said. What the hell are you working on. You don't even have a fucking job. His eyes were closed again.

I'm doing a website, Dwight said. He wondered if he should say more. He hadn't mentioned anything to Darcy about the new New Seep, the razing of the town, his involvement in the protest. He said, I saw our house moving down the highway.

Darcy grunted. Then he said, What. In a dream.

No, Dwight said. Our house from Seep. They moved it. It passed by me on Highway 22.

Yeah, Darcy said.

They're tearing down Seep, Dwight said. They moved the whole town. They're going to build some sort of recreation town.

I heard about that, Darcy said. His voice was thick with near-sleep.

I belong to a group. We're trying to stop what's going on, Dwight said.

Yeah, Darcy said. I heard.

He folded his hands over his belly. His chest sunk into a slow and steady rhythm. Dwight swivelled his chair and clicked the poker-room bookmark on his computer. He was into his second hand when Darcy spoke again: I got a surprise for you. Dwight watched a player make a big bet after the flop. He had a pair of fours in the hole, but the board was showing a lot of faces. He folded.

What surprise, Dwight said.

If I told you, Darcy said. But he didn't finish the sentence. He slept in the recliner. Dwight continued playing for a couple of hours. He was only down $60 when he called it a night.

Over the next few days, Dwight continued to build the website. He posted a blurb that Len from the Wilderness Foundation sent him, detailing the plants and animals that frequented the townsite. Len had included a photo of a tiny fern, whose only known habitat outside the

Precambrian Shield was along the river between the two dams, clinging to the crevices in the rock along the cliff face. In the photo, a nickel, beaver-side up, demonstrated its size — the coin could cover the whole plant. I've probably peed on this, Dwight thought as he posted the photo to the home page of the website. My father's ashes. Walter from the reserve sent him an interview with his grandmother, who claimed her grandfather had opposed the transfer of the band territory to Prairie Mountain Light & Power in 1905. The tidbit about the transfer price being a dozen horses, given to band council as payment, was repeated. Though Walter's grandmother also conceded that her grandfather accepted a gift of tobacco and six blankets. In his write-up, Walter called it "hush money." Dwight gave the interview its own page. Dr. van Barneveld from the university and Water Conservation Advocacy Group submitted a detailed and impenetrable analysis of the proposed plan to tap into the underground aquifer and pipe water to the valley. The title: Borrowing from Peter to Pay Paul. He included a number of charts and diagrams, all in black and white. It too got its own page, but no matter how much Dwight played with the format and sizing, it was a mass of text and data that scrolled on for screen after screen. He was taken aback one day when his email notification pinged: You have New Mail from Smithson, Morton Francis <smithson @smithsonandco.com>

> Dear Mr. Eliot—
> I have been informed by Willow Howse that you are the
> keeper of the web presence for the Coalition for Assured
> Responsible Development, who are organizing opposition
> to the former PMP&L lands out at Seep.

Dwight touched the bridge of his nose, felt the bump in the cartilage there. Smithson was retired, but his name still graced one of the most prestigious law firms in town — one of the last not merged with national and international practices. Dwight read on with trepidation. Smithson's career was built on service to the resource industry, and Dwight expected some sort of cease and desist order.

> Ms. Howse suggested I forward the attached brief prepared on behalf of the Committee of Concerned Ranchers and Ratepayers of Sheepshorn Municipal District. You can post it, but please ensure it is attributed to the committee as a whole and not me personally. I am sure I can trust you to respect this confidentiality, Mr. Eliot.

> Thank you for your co-operation
> Smithson

Dwight opened the attachment and scanned it. The concerned ranchers and ratepayers made the argument that intensifying urban or exurban development, adding several thousand townies (and wealthy ones at that), would skew the tax base and political orientation of Sheepshorn M.D.. While recognizing a town might bring more tax revenue, the ranchers and ratepayers worried that the traditional rural concerns — water management, road maintenance, and civic representation — would erode. The email had a postscript:

> P.S. It is indeed a small world.
> — S.

He had not seen Sara since the day she went off to the Stampede ten years ago; had not spoken to her since the telephone call to Dusty's; had never encountered Smithson since the night he head-butted Dwight. He had never talked to Darcy about it — there were a lot of things he and Darcy never brought up.

★ ★ ★

The day in mid-July that he drove down to see his mother in the Crowsnest Pass, Dwight Eliot was a singular man. As he headed down the sweep of the hill into the Waldron Community Pasture on Highway 22, alone in his '97 Corolla, he did not reflect on all the cars he ever owned, all the men he ever was and ever would be. In his mind, he played over and over the second interview he had conducted with Laugh Jack. Ten years ago this very day. His mother was taking a nap when he arrived and he sat in a chair in the small room she shared with a woman who was in a persistent vegetative state. He rarely saw his mother in this room — usually when he visited, they met in the lodge's lounge, where she preferred to pass her muted days. He watched her sleep, listened to the uncanny breathing through her tracheostoma. When she stirred, he made a point of clearing his throat and shifting in his seat so that she would not be surprised. She reached to her bedside table and retrieved her glasses, then turned to look at him. Hi, Mom, Dwight said.

She pulled a pad and pencil from her housecoat pocket, and scribbled a note: It's not even Sunday. The afternoon light spilled around the edges of the drawn drapes, giving enough light to read her writing.

Everyday is Sunday when I don't have a job, he said. And Monday. Tuesday. Friday.

I know the feeling, she wrote in a note. But you have to try to keep track. Then she scribbled another message: It took me years. But if you don't keep track you give up.

She scratched some more with her pencil. You haven't been here for weeks. Even Darcy and his girlfriend have been here. Is everything OK?

I talked to Laugh Jack, Dwight said. His mother gave him a queer look, and scribbled. With a Ouija board? she wrote.

No. When he was alive. Ten years ago, Dwight said. They sat in the stillness of the room. Then she scratched a question. Why now?

Why talk about it now, Dwight said. His mother nodded, and shrugged. And why have I never talked about it before. Another shrug.

I didn't know what to say, Dwight said. He gave me a pretty detailed story about what happened that day. At least with you.

His mother wrote furiously. She filled two pages of her notebook, looked at what she had marked down, and stuffed the pages in her pocket. She wrote something else and passed it to Dwight: LJ didn't know anything.

I think he was carrying a torch for you, mom, Dwight said.

One word on the paper: FOOL.

That's harsh, Dwight said. He may have been a bit eccentric. Weird, even. But I don't think he was foolish.

Ellie shook her head, then pointed to herself. You're the fool, Dwight said. Then she pointed at him. I'm the fool, he said. She nodded, then shook her head again, and held up her hand so her finger and thumb were a half inch apart. A little bit, Dwight said. She tapped her head with the pencil she held in her other hand. He was a little bit crazy, Dwight said, but his voice was unsure.

She shook her head, rolled her eyes, finally wrote a note: LJ only knew a little about me.

Dwight fidgeted with the paper. He knew there were problems between you and dad, Dwight said. She opened her hands up, cocked her head, as if to say, everyone knew that. What else is there to know, Dwight said.

She wrote some more: Once upon a time, I promised you a letter.

You've got a letter for me, Dwight said. She shook her head, then mimed the act of writing. You will write one now, Dwight said. She put a mark on the paper and showed it to him: Soon. Then she added Very before it. She tucked the notepad in her pocket and swung her legs off the bed to indicate the conversation was over.

They made their way to the lounge. She was still spry, but allowed herself to rest against Dwight and held his arm as they walked. When they settled, Dwight told her about seeing the old house on the road, about the protests at Seep, about Darcy staying at his house. She wrote in her notepad: Yes, I got a visit from Willow.

Dwight smiled. Of course Willow had visited. Ellie was her Grandmother after all. His mother wrote something else, looked at it. Shook her head, and stowed the words in her pocket.

Dwight asked if she was interested in coming to the picnic next month. It'll be the day before my birthday, Dwight said. We can celebrate. You can see what they're doing. Ellie mimed laughter, then wrote a note. I'll stay here, but I'll think about you. She added a word: Darcy? I don't want him there, Dwight said.

As he drove away in the bright midsummer evening, he drummed his fingers on the money in his pocket. He thought about all the letters he had ever written and received and would write and receive. And he went to the casino.

He came home another day and a car he didn't recognize was parked in front of the house — a Smart car. He was coming from an appointment with his outplacement counsellor at PeopleFirst!, who was urging him to start a consulting business. Tap into that market for freelance assistant corporate archivists. He had made a stop at Centre City Casino on his way home. A wad of twenty-dollar bills made a bulge in his front pocket. When he got to the house he heard a woman's laugh drift through the open kitchen window from the backyard. An honest, deep laughter.

Out on the deck, he was shocked to see Willow sitting with Darcy. The washtub firepit was blazing, even though it was a hot sunny day. To the west and north, clouds were piling up, promising thunder and lightning later. Darcy and Willow occupied a pair of Muskoka-style chairs that Darcy had fashioned from the kits he had convinced Dwight to buy at Home Depot when they were building the deck. Each had a glass of iced tea perched on the flat arm of a chair. A glass pitcher of the beverage sweated on a low bench — more crudely knocked together by Darcy from odds and ends left over from the construction project. Uncle Dwight, Willow said. Darcy was just telling me funny stories about you two growing up in Seep.

Grab a seat, little buddy, Darcy said, waving his arm expansively. He knocked his drink over, spilling the tea, but he shot his hand out and caught the glass in mid-fall, halfway to the ground. Wow. Did you see that, Darcy said. Like a fu —, he stopped himself, then continued — like a goddamned cat. Like that Russian goalie, Tic-tac.

Tretiak, Dwight said. Vladislav Tretiak.

Tic-tac, Tretiak, paddywhack, Darcy said. He looked at his daughter Willow. Isn't this guy something with the details, he said, nodding towards Dwight. Willow looked from brother to brother. She was smiling her brilliant wide grin, but her brow was ever so slightly knit.

Dwight stood at the back door. Then he closed it, and grabbed one of the aluminum lawn chairs leaning against the house.

I was just telling my girl here about the time you threw a handful of spoons at my head, Darcy said. Then you lit out the front door and I come chasing you. But you had figured the whole thing out. You got your shoes on, I'm in my bare feet. In the winter. And you run around the back door, lock it, then lock the front door. I'm goddamn freezing my can off. Darcy turned to Willow. And the little bastard won't let me in.

Does Amy know you're here, Dwight said to Willow, ignoring his brother's anecdote.

Or how's about that time you half fell out of that big fir, grew down by the cliff, Darcy said. Your collar catches that one branch. The top buttons come flying off but not the last couple. And you're just hanging there by your neck.

Willow, Dwight said.

You're just kicking your feet and clawing at your neck, Darcy said. He used his hands to mime a man choking. Turning six shades of blue.

Actually, Willow said to Dwight. I came to talk to you. She smoothed her cotton summer dress where it draped over her knees.

And — . She shrugged. Grandma told me Darcy was staying here. So I thought I'd drop by instead of calling on the phone.

So anyways, I come over and grab a foot, Darcy said. Give it a yank. The last button pops off and you come crashing down. You land flat on your back. By now Darcy was standing, acting out the parts. Knocked the wind outta you. Your eyes roll back and you go all limp. I can see you're not fucking breathing. You make a sick sound. Darcy mimics a sound like he's got something stuck in his throat. And I think, I save the little fucker from choking and now he breaks his fucking neck. Then you take a big gulp of air and sit right up. Halle-fucking-luiah.

Darcy, Dwight said.

Darcy sat back down. Excuse my English, he said. He brought the glass to his mouth, realized it was empty, set it down on the bench. Good thing you weren't any higher in that tree, Darcy said.

Willow, does Amy know Darcy is in town, Dwight said. Does she know you came here today.

Shirt's probably still in the tree, Darcy said.

The tree is still there, Willow said to Darcy. A huge Douglas fir.

Jesus Christ, Dwight said.

They sat without speaking. A woodpecker began tapping at a utility pole in the lane. A car alarm sounded for a few seconds then went silent. Somewhere, in a backyard close by, children shrieked and offered their indistinct voices to the wind. The white noise of traffic on Glenmore Trail a few blocks away filled in the gaps in sound.

Man, you really know how to harsh a guy's mellow, Darcy said.

Willow laughed, a full spontaneous utterance that responded to an unexpected delight. Oh Darcy, she said. That sounds so weird coming from you. Darcy looked at her, scowling as if his feelings were hurt, while at the same time betraying a sheepish grin.

Dwight took a big breath, then expelled it. Not quite a sigh, but a release nonetheless. What the hell, he said. God grant me the serenity.

Amen, brother, Darcy said. Serenity prayer. Let's do the twelve-step boogaloo. That's what I told Willow last week when I called her. Ninth step. Make amends.

You called her, Dwight said. I thought she just popped by. To see me.

Darcy poured himself more iced tea. Well, mom sent me a note. With her number. He took a pull from his glass. I told you I had a surprise, Darcy said, and winked broadly at his brother.

I didn't know you were in the program, Dwight said.

Darcy waved his hand dismissively. In the program. Out of the program, he said. Twelve steps. Two-steps. All the steps. I've been up and down those stairs a dozen times. Try a hundred and forty-four steps. A gross of steps. Some gross steps, that's for sure. Today, it's step nine. He looked at Willow. I've done a lot of bad shit. I hurt a lot of people. I'm sorry if I hurt you, Darcy said. And your mom. Amy. I got her pregnant, walked away, and never looked back. I'm sorry for that. I did a lot of really bad shit. Bad people. Good people. I fucked 'em all over. Maybe it's a good thing you weren't around. Today, for today, I wanna say, I'm back. Here I am. Your dad. Warts and all. Doing the best I can with what I got. Which ain't much.

Dwight watched his brother as he spoke. A welter of conflicting emotions arose in his throat. He thought he might gag, spew right here on the deck. He hadn't eaten since early this morning. There was nothing to bring up. He wasn't sure if he was going to barf from disgust or some weird empathy. Tears brimmed in Darcy's eyes. The bastard's believing his own hype, Dwight thought. What about making amends for me — for the years of betrayal, for a dead dog, for Sara, for Julee. Dwight hadn't talked to his own daughter for ten years. He had a son in France who sent a Christmas card once a year. And Dwight didn't send one back. Dwight's own face bloomed red with shame. How can you make amends when I can't make amends?

Ah Darcy — Dad, Willow said. She moved from her seat and went to her father. Awkwardly, she leaned into him, and Darcy reached for her. He tossed his iced tea aside, this time letting it fall to the ground where it spilled and the tumbler rolled in a lazy semicircle. They embraced. When they were both seated again, they spent some time composing themselves, wiping at their eyes.

The nausea passed for Dwight. He discovered he had stuck his hand in his pocket, where he held it flat against the fold of money there. A fraught slab. Something solid against his thigh. Tonight, he would go to the casino and play roulette. What is my lucky number today, he thought.

The three of them sat in the heat. The woodpecker pecked. The children shouted. A slow-moving bumblebee lumbered through the space between them. Darcy picked up his glass, and filled it again. She called me dad, he said. More waterworks. They settled. Dwight came out of his stillness. Darcy and Willow found a fragile rhythm. The three of them discussed the upcoming First Last Great Seep Country Action Picnic.

Why action, Dwight asked. Willow explained that some of the political activists attached to CARD wanted to call it "day of action." It's going to be a great big celebration, Willow said. Some ranchers are bringing horses. The band members are going to set-up a lodge and a bannock booth. The environmentalists are going to take people on nature walks.

Hey, I got an idea, Darcy said. We should do something at that big tree.

What tree, Dwight said.

The fuc—, I mean the big tree you damn near hung yourself by the neck until dead, Darcy said. It's still there, right Willow?

They agreed that was a good idea. Dwight asked Willow if the media was on board. A couple of TV stations had said they would send remotes, but you never knew with them. If they showed up at the wrong time of day, like when they were setting up, it might not make very good news. But a couple of print media were interested. A reporter from the *Herald* had been covering some of the preparations, and she'd be there all day.

A local reporter for one of the national papers thought there was possibility for a feature, so was planning to be there. A pair of women documentary filmmakers were trying to roundup funding and a crew to come out on the day — they're doing a project on land use in western Canada.

They talked about security. Dwight asked Willow if she had been talking to her mother, if she knew what the plans of the developer were. Would they try to throw everybody off the land? Were the police going to be involved?

They know the media's going to be there, Willow said. So they're going to play it cool. Somebody will be there, watching us. The cops will drop by for sure. Actually, we've asked them to come by.

I can be security, Darcy said. Like the Angels at Altamont.

I don't think that's a good example, Dwight said. They killed a guy.

Guy probably deserved it, Darcy said. Getting in Keef Richards' face.

Not a good idea, Dwight said. The guy was just a fan. The biker just went crazy.

Guys, Willow said. I don't think we'll need bouncers, Darcy.

Just sayin', Darcy said. I'm here if you need me.

Willow shuffled through the papers she had brought. She handed Dwight a copy of the poster, a few pages of notes, and a thumb drive on a lanyard. For the website, she said.

And the activists, Dwight said. Are they anarchists? What are they going to do. Wear balaclavas and throw stones or worse.

Oh Uncle Dwight, Willow said. They're organizing a puppet parade.

Puppets, Dwight said.

Hey, Darcy said. A parade to the big tree. Ring around the rosie with huge effing puppets.

And singing, Willow said.

I could bring my guitar, Darcy said.

My guitar, Dwight said.

Darcy looked over at him. Only because I sold it to you twenty-five years ago, Darcy said.

I rest my case, Dwight said.

Well, Willow said. We don't have a sound system.

No problem, Darcy said. I know how to do that. I was a roadie once. Lots of times. Big shows, too. I did a Crowbar tour. I got this covered.

We don't really have the money — we'd need a generator, cords, speakers, microphones, maybe even a stage, Willow said. Somebody already looked into it. It's more money than you think.

Darcy jumped up. Let me show you guys something, he said. He went over to a box he had built into a corner of the deck. He lifted the lid, moved the few things that were in it — a croquet set that had never been out of the box, a coil of hose, an extension cord — then reached in and came out with some of the deck boards that had been fashioned into a kind of a cover. Darcy looked over at them. Secret compartment, Darcy said. He lifted an object wrapped in a green garbage bag from the recess under the deck and brought it over. He unwrapped a knapsack from the bag. Feast your eyes on this he said. He unzipped the big pocket of the knapsack and turned it upside down. Bricks of money, hundred-dollar bills, twenties, even fives and tens spilled onto the deck. Each brick was secured with two thick elastics.

Dwight felt the bile rise in his throat again. Jesus Christ, he said. No. No way.

What is that, Willow said. She had her hand at her neck.

What does it look like, Darcy said. Money. Doh-re-mi. Green. Cold hard. Then he lowered his voice to a hoarse whisper. A hundred and six-teen thousand dollars. Give or take.

Dwight went into the house. He ran off a glass of water from the kitchen sink. He listened to the voices in the yard. It's clean, Darcy said. I didn't have to do anything. Just be friends with this old guy in the joint. He gave it to me.

Willow said something Dwight couldn't hear.

No, no, Darcy said. Look, I can score the PA and sound set-up. You

179

can get those lesbos or whatever to do a movie. They need some funds. Look at this pile.

I never said they were lesbians, Willow said.

But they are, right, Darcy said.

Dwight went back outside. Willow was gathering her papers and her things. I don't think we can use this money, Darcy, she said. I mean, I appreciate the gesture. But I just can't take it.

Oh c'mon, Darcy said. I just blew my secret for this. I'm telling you, it's completely legit. He was stuffing the bills back into his bag. I was nice to this old guy. That's all. I had his back. A long-timer. Nobody paid shit attention to him. He was croaking of fucking cancer, man. Had nobody left on the inside or the outside. He just needed someone. One night he tells me where he's got this stash, tells me if he croaks before he kills his number that I should take it. He fucking died. Fucking lung cancer. He fucking gave it to me and now I want to fucking give it to you. Willow was holding her purse in her arms, clutching it across her chest. Fuck, Darcy said. He pushed the package back into its hiding place. Fuck. Darcy slammed the things back into the deck box and crashed the lid down.

I can't, Willow said. I think I better go now.

Go, Darcy said. Just fucking go. He fumbled for a cigarette from his package and lit it. I just wanted to do some fucking good, for once. Willow turned. Willow, Darcy said. You can't tell nobody.

Dwight walked Willow to her car. They were speechless. When she was behind the wheel and turned the ignition, Dwight said, I'll call you. Or email you. Willow nodded. She looked straight ahead, over the steering wheel. It'll be OK, Dwight said. She nodded again, but couldn't look at him.

Back in the house, Darcy was in the front room. The house was hot, sweltering from the midday heat. Don't you say a fucking word or I'll fucking pound the shit out of your smart-ass head, Darcy said. Don't say a fucking word. Darcy lit another smoke. Dwight opened his mouth to say something but Darcy cut him off. If you tell me to stop smoking, I'll put this fucking butt out in your fucking eye. And I'll make you eat the fucking thing. The tobacco smoke lifted into the air of the room. Dwight imagined he could hear it settling into the paint, the furniture, the drapes. When he finished smoking, Darcy went to the kitchen and doused the end in the sink. Don't you fucking move, he said when he left the room.

When he came back, he began to talk, pacing the small floor space. What a fuck-up, Darcy said. Who turns their back on that kind of cash. I fucked up. He looked at Dwight. Did you hear what she said. She fucking called me dad. Then I fucked up and it was Darcy again. Don't say a fucking word. Darcy had his hand clenched in a fist. He was looking for something to punch. He went to the door and slammed it shut. Then he slammed his hand into the wood of the jamb. He bloodied his knuckles.

It was like I said, Darcy said. The old fucker gave it to me. He knew he was done for. I looked out for him, watched his back in the joint. It was my fucking chance. That's why I came here. This was my fucking chance. Get clean. Sober fucking up. Buy some fucking corner store or some shit. A little business. Just fucking fade the fuck away, like a fucking citizen.

He was sitting now. He lit another cigarette. Dwight coughed, tried to stifle it, coughed again. Give me a break, Darcy said. He looked at Dwight and stabbed the cigarette in the air as he spoke. OK. It's like this. The cat's out of the bag. You tell anybody about this and I'll fucking have you for dinner. Capeesh? Dwight nodded. You got to talk to Willow and tell her no one, I mean no fucking body, can know about this. This dough is clean, but there are some people. They find out I got scratch they'll fucking come for it.

Dwight nodded again. His hand was in his pocket on his own wad of bills. She called me dad, Darcy said. Then this. Darcy looked Dwight square in the eye. It stays where it is, Darcy said. You won't lay a finger on it.

Darcy, Dwight said. Darcy sucked on his smoke. Don't fall off the wagon.

Fuck you, Darcy said.

Listen. Dwight said. Don't do something stupid. You start using, it'll all be gone, and you will too.

Shut up and let me think, Darcy said. He wet a thumb and forefinger and pinched out the coal on his smoke. This is my one fucking shot, Darcy said. I don't need your pep talk. You know, I was gonna tell you. I wanted you to help me. Like invest it or something.

You're barking up the wrong tree, Dwight said. I'm not so hot with that.

I'm gonna leave it right where it is, Darcy said. He moved in close, and grabbed Dwight around the nape of his neck, pulling them together until their foreheads touched. You know where it is. If anything happens to me, you do the right thing. He lightly tapped Dwight's forehead with his own. He broke the clasp.

What are you going to do? Dwight said.

I don't fucking know, Darcy said. He went downstairs, and in a few minutes Dwight heard the guitar as Darcy began strafing through the rock 'n' roll riff catalogue. God grant me, Dwight thought. He swept up the cigarette butt from where Darcy had left it on the table, got a cloth and wiped the table down. He went to the office and checked email, checked the betting line for the baseball games that night. He jingled his car keys and brushed a thumb over the bulge in his front pocket. He left, stopping at the 7-Eleven to buy two hundred dollars worth of Sport Select tickets, then drove all the way out to the casino near Seep. By the time he was halfway there lightning began to scratch the sky and thunder roared. There was rain, then he pulled over on the shoulder under an overpass and let a swath of hail pass. By the time he reached the casino it was getting near dark. He decided his lucky number was ten.

It was.

The day your father died I came into the house and found him passed out on the rug in the living room. It was the middle of the afternoon and I hadn't seen him for three or four days. His feet were bare and filthy. His pants were muddy from the knees down. He had urinated in them and the half-dried piss stained the crotch. There was a splotch of what looked like dried blood on his shirt pocket, and a small dark stain at the corner of his mouth. I sat in the chair in the corner and watched him snore. Every two or three minutes he would stop breathing. Alcoholic apnea. Then his chest would heave and he would explode with a glottal heave and start snoring again. Once, a pink bubble flew from his nose and popped. Then suddenly he sat up. He lolled his head and I came into his focus.

16.

The Wheel Spun

14 August 2009

At the casino, the afternoon before the picnic, Dwight set himself at roulette. At this early hour, he was the only player in a seat, but they opened a table for him — management knew him as a serious player. The only other action was cards — blackjack, Caribbean stud, mini baccarat, and the poker room. But the cards had been brutal the last few days, everything had been brutal, and he didn't feel up to the social interaction of Texas Hold'em. They wouldn't open craps till later. The wheel and the bouncing ball had the right pace for this day, clacking out a rhythm just for him. The action was steady but not too fast. He decided his number was twenty-five, and he played various systems and strategies around it, betting it straight up, the splits, the corners, street bets, dozens, columns, the high numbers, the odd numbers. He lost steadily. He had been losing steadily for two weeks, burning through thousands of dollars.

Today, he tried different money-management angles, letting rare wins ride for a bet, skimming profit from even rarer instances where he had two winners or partial winners on back-to-back spins. For the first hour or more, the only words spoken by him or the dealer or the croupier were, No more bets, the call of winning numbers, and the calls to the pit boss when the dealer sold Dwight another $100 or $200 worth of chips. An older couple sat down after a while. After a few plays, Dwight had them pegged as retirees, probably in a motorhome parked in the RV section of the lot where the casino offered hookups and the buffet breakfast for $29.95 a night. They were tanned from chasing the sun, the man's face and neck like a well-worn leather wallet, the woman's hands and forearms splotched with pigment too big to call freckles but not big enough to call liver spots. They sported matching crisp white sun visors, colourful open-neck golf shirts (his, pale green; hers, pastel purple) and pressed white shorts with cuffs at the knees. They each had bright Nike crosstrainers, she with ankle socks, he with tube socks halfway up his calves. The socks were marked with the famous swoosh too.

The man had no idea what he was doing, and tossed down random bets, numbers straight up and unrelated splits, and covering zero and double-zero with one dollar bets every spin. The woman played a tighter game, working different angles on the 7-8-9 street. They were playing fifty-cent chits to Dwight's two-dollar ones. But they started to win. The man collected two bets in a row from his zero-bet gambits, then the woman hit two more, one after the other.

Poppa needs a new pair of shoes, the man said. Going to live large tonight, eh, Beth.

Oh Bill, the woman said. Stop showing off. It doesn't become you.

The man looked to Dwight, shot a conspiratorial wink, as if to say, Watch this. Lucky in cards, lucky in love, the man said.

Oh Bill, the woman said. Dwight could see it coming. The man was a talker. He would start up a conversation. The casino was an extension of his living room or office, of a life spent selling automotive components to strangers.

The wheel spun, the ball dropped into the track and whirred. As it dropped lower, the dealer called, No more bets. The white orb popped and danced then settled on its number. Eight. The woman won again.

The man let out a holler — Yee-haw. The woman allowed herself a pleased smile. The croupier put a dolly on the winner and raked in the other bets, including the piles down at Dwight's end. The woman kept winning, and her luck attracted some more players.

Hey, tough luck down there, my friend, the man said to Dwight.

Bill, the woman said. It's not polite to comment on another's position. She sounded like she was reading from a book of etiquette. You'll have to pardon my husband, the woman said to Dwight. He's not much of a gamesman.

Dwight resigned himself to the inevitable. They were retirees, they did have a motorhome, they did follow the sun. The man had been in sales — not car parts, but machine tooling equipment for aerospace components.

Bill helped put the men on the moon, the woman said.

Now Beth, the man said.

And the space shuttles, she said. But not those o-rings. Or the tiles, the woman said.

He was one of the lucky ones, retired with a good pension before NASA went to hell in a handbasket. They were from the U.S., so Dwight didn't have to say much. He noticed that when Americans and Canadians met in situations like these — in the casino, on airplanes — the Americans were happy to talk about themselves and uncurious if the Canadians chose to be reticent. They were from Indiana, though they called Arizona home now, not that they had much more than a post office box there. There were more losing spins for him, winners for the couple. The ball didn't want to land on any number greater than eighteen. Dwight bought more chips, emptying his pockets of the last of the bills he carried — nearly $600. He had been carrying over $8,000 just two days ago.

What about you, young man, the woman said. Up till now she'd let the husband do the talking.

I'm just killing some time before I do something tomorrow, Dwight said.

And what would that be, the woman said. Not more gambling, I hope.

He allowed himself a smile. He bet on twenty-five, the splits and the corners. I thought it wasn't polite to comment on another's position, Dwight said. The woman blushed. It's OK, Dwight said.

Well, she said. What *are* you doing tomorrow.

I'm going to a picnic, he said.

That sounds like fun, she said. Where is that. In the national park, I bet.

No more bets, the dealer said.

No, Dwight said. It's just over on the other side of the highway.

A community picnic, she said.

The ball bounced and settled. Thirty-two. The croupier raked in his chips.

An ex-community, he said. And he found himself telling these strangers about Seep, about the day he was born, about seeing his house on the highway, about losing his job, about his drug-addicted brother, about the day that was planned to save Seep from further development. He had a couple of winners as he talked, his pile grew, and he kept talking. Then more losing spins.

That's the damnedest story, the man said. You were born in a ball diamond. Isn't that the damnedest story, Beth.

We went to Alaska, the woman said. Then we came south for the Perseids. This was the best year in a long time for the Perseids. We had to come south for the night sky. There's too much daytime in Alaska. We were in Jasper.

They were quite a show, the man said. We drove up to the icefields and sat up half the night. Just last Wednesday was the peak. Dozens of shooting stars every hour.

The ball dropped on the nine. The woman won again.

I'll be damned, the man said.

I'll be right back, Dwight said. He went to an automated teller machine and took a cash advance on his MasterCard. He maxed it out. When he returned to the table the couple were getting ready to leave.

The man looked at the sheaf of bills Dwight held ready in his hand. Maybe you should call it an evening, son, the man said. It's not really rolling your way.

Oh, Bill, the woman said.

We'd be happy to fix you some supper in the unit, the man said. Maybe go on over to that picnic of yours tomorrow.

Dwight was already counting the bills on the felt. The dealer changed the money, called to the pit boss: One thousand.

Thanks for the offer, but I'm OK, Dwight said. He set his new stacks in front of him, began clapping his tokens on twenty-five and its neighbours. The couple left. Dwight gambled and lost. He lost. And he lost and he lost and he lost until he had nothing.

Ellie, he gurgled. Then he coughed and a great geyser of blood splashed on his shirt front. He rolled onto all fours. And coughed another gout. Then he stopped coughing and just opened his mouth and blood poured forth. I could see that with each beat of his heart the blood pulsed out. He started to make choking sounds and his arms gave out and he collapsed on the rug. But still he wheezed and bled, the blood now frothy as he struggled for air around the gush of hemorrhaging. And I sat in the chair and watched until I could see that his chest wasn't heaving anymore. But for another minute the blood continued to pool, until finally I knew his heart had stopped. I rose from the chair, and careful to step around the gore, I went to the phone in the kitchen and called the ambulance. I think my husband is dead, I told them. He was fifty-one years old. You were ten.

17.

Picnic

8 August 2009

"Now" eclipses "once upon a time." The imperfect past collapses into a continuous present, predicting future perfect. Alone, Dwight drove the few miles from the casino hotel where he had the spent the night — playing roulette till his money ran out at 2:00 AM, then a short sleep scrunched in the back seat of his Toyota — and arrived with the rosy-fingered dawn. As the sun rose, the light slid down the slope of the ridges to the west. The day would be hot and blue, but now the August morning air hinted at approaching autumn — too dry for a dew, yet cool and moist. As the temperature rose through the day, the relative humidity would drop, and skin would parch. A bare breeze soughed through the aspens, setting the brittle leaves atremble. High above, a passenger jet winged east towards the city, bittering the sky.

In the now overgrown ball field, Dwight planted himself where he had sprouted. Seep, New Seep, Next Seep. I was born there, he said to the grasshoppers awakening at his feet, and pointed to a spot to his left. I grew up over there, he said to a passing sparrow, gesturing behind the bluff of trees to where he knew a gouge in the earth marked a spot where home once was, where a clean square on the bare pine-board floor once marked the absence of the rug; the sparrow swerved and flew off that way, as if taking heed. My father died there, he said to the bird. He kicked at a clod of volunteer daisies growing among the knee-high crabgrass and foxtails. I killed a dog over there, he said. Dwight walked to where he had parked and began removing items from the trunk of the Toyota — pamphlets that Willow had asked him to pick up at the printer, six flats of bottled water he bought at Costco, some copies of the PML&P photo of the grease pencil overwriting the river that he turned into postcards. He stashed them by the service road that demarcated the space between the edge of the field and the slope of the riverbank, where the CARD would be setting up. Then he got in his car and drove back to the casino. He had maxed his credit cards the day before, but still had some cash in his chequing account after he had taken the daily limit. He was back to the picnic in less than two hours.

As the morning bloomed, people began to arrive. Willow in her Smart car led a convoy of protesters in their Priuses, Volkswagens, and a waste-vegetable-oil-burning, right-hand drive Mitsubishi Delica van. These were the vanguard, the volunteers who organized food and information booths, who set up shade canopies for a first aid station, unloaded propane barbecues and coolers. Over by the turnoff from the main road, people were erecting a teepee. Later in the afternoon, pickups from the reserve and the ranches would show up, some towing horse trailers, along with carloads of curious families drawn by the promise of free picnicking and an old-fashioned summer fair that had been touted in the newspapers, posted on websites, even via Facebook and Twitter. Amy showed up mid-morning in her company truck, uniformed, radio on hip. Boadicea bounded across the field, zigging and zagging but then settling on Willow. Amy ambled without haste after her dog, then hugged her daughter.

Hey girl, Amy said.

Hi mom, Willow said. She laughed. It's going to be a good day. Two more trucks pulled in and parked near Amy's. One was a luxury truck, a Cadillac Escalade, unmarked; the other a crew cab with the SmarTec logo on the door. I see the generals have arrived, Willow said. She watched as Simon Love and his magnificent jacket got out from behind the wheel of the Cadillac along with another man duded out in shiny boots and shinier denims. From the back seat emerged two younger men in uniforms that matched Amy's. From the crew cab a quartet of consultants in khakis and matching SmarTec windbreakers emerged. They set to work unloading their own gear — more information, a barbecue, coolers, and some video equipment.

Is it a problem that you're over here. Talking to me, Willow said.

No, Amy said. I've been designated the go-between. You know, I'm a little bit of everything — a little bit Indian, a little bit white, a little bit the local girl, got my daughter with the other side, got a friendly dog, I know CPR.

Aw, mom, Willow said. Everything is going to be cool.

I know, Amy said. These guys have decided to play along. As she spoke, a five-ton flatbed truck pulled in, with a half-dozen portable toilets as payload. Look, they're even kicking in with the portable biffies.

Willow cracked a grin and let out another laugh. Oh my god, Willow said. That is so much a lifesaver. We talked about this. Jordan and Jared are off in the bush digging pit latrines. Willow looked over as the operator of the flatbed started to sling the toilets one at a time. Simon Love caught Willow's eye, and gestured to the toilets, then gave a formal little bow, as if to say, My pleasure.

Willow, Amy said. I'm really proud of you.

But mom, it's not me, Willow said. Then she interrupted herself to call out to a young man walking by with a spade: Jordan! Jordan! You can stop digging. The cavalry's arrived. Then Willow turned again to her mom. I'm just one voice here.

I know, Amy said. But you're my daughter. It's your voice I hear. So I'm proud of you, not these other clowns.

We're not clowns, Willow said. This is important to a lot of people. Jordan and Jared came ambling over. They looked like twins with their dreadlocks and baggy Goodwill pants, except that Jordan was black and Jared was carrot-topped.

I didn't mean it like that, Amy said. Just — Amy nodded to Jordan and Jared. Shrugged.

Well, how did you mean it? Willow said.

I'm proud of you.

Are we just clowning around to you? Her posture tensed. Why is it always two steps forward and one step backwards with you?

I hope you can change this.

Me and my clowns, Willow said.

Yes, Amy said.

Um, Willow, Jordan said, can we talk a minute about the toilets.

What, Willow said. Her voice was sharp.

Some of us don't want to use those ones they brought, Jared said. Like, why should we take anything from those capitalist fuckers.

We already dug two perfectly good holes, Jordan said. Who needs a fucking plastic company shitter?

I think I better go, Amy said. Good luck, Willow. She turned and walked toward the corporate workers. Here Bodie, c'mon girl, she called, and Boadicea came running from where she was nosing the coolers in the shade.

Dude, who was that, Jordan said.

That was my mother, Willow said. The comprador.

That's fucked, Jared said.

Not really, Willow said. Just what it is. She looked at her latrine patrol. She loosened her shoulders and broke into one of her disarming smiles. Listen, if you clowns want to do your business in the woods, that's cool with me. But my guess is not everyone will be comfortable with that. Are you cool if some of us compromise with the enemy and use the biffies?

What's a biffy, Jordan said.

Yeah, double-u tee eff, Jared said.

The porta-potties, Willow said.

I dunno, Jordan said. The two young men looked at each other, as if communicating telepathically. Then they spoke simultaneously: I guess it's cool to use 'em, Jordan said.

We'll boycott 'em on principle, Jared said.

They looked at each other again.

Split decision, Willow said. Listen, she said, I have a thousand things to do here. Maybe you guys can talk to some of the others and see what they think. See if you can figure out a consensus. They agreed and set off, shovels on their shoulders.

The schedule of events for the day was loosely organized around a parade that was to start at 3:00 PM, march to the teepee, wend its way past the power plant, along the bank of the river, past a few of the destroyed streets and end at the field. Then there would be some speeches. This was all designed to allow any media to cover the event and get the reports back to the city for the 6:00 PM news. After the speeches, the coalition would serve up beef and beans and vegetarian food for supper — the beef supplied by the ranchers, the tofu and salads by an organic market whose owner was vice-president of the Wilderness Foundation. The evening was more or less unstructured, with the only programmed event being a lantern festival after sunset. This last event had been a bone of contention — many of the organizers, Willow included, argued that everyone should just go home after the evening meal, while there was still light. But many of the younger folks, the hippies, the anarchists, the environmentalists, the agitprop puppeteers, were beholden to the idea of welcoming the night with candles and a coming together of light and people. At one of the meetings a woman had showed slides and videos of a lantern festival on Vancouver Island in which she had participated. Even Dwight had to admit it looked like a spectacular and soothing event.

In mid-afternoon, Dwight volunteered to run into Malcolm to pick up more flats of water. When he returned, a police car was parked at the entrance to the townsite. Across the road from them, drumbeats and singing rang out from a dancing circle by the teepee. Two RCMP members leaned against the hood of the car and waved as he drove in. One of them held a clipboard and Dwight saw him checking licence tags and making notes. He dropped the water at a concession table then tried to find a spot for his Toyota. One end of the field was jammed with cars parked willy-nilly, and more vehicles perched in a line on the shoulder of the service road. He drove past the field designated for parking and turned down the rutted track that was the remnant of the street he grew up on. Empty spaces marked the places where houses had once been. Some still bore gaping holes to mark the cellars; others had been smoothed over, but their freshly turned earth looked like newly covered graves. At a couple of sites, piles of lumber designated the houses too dilapidated to bother moving. They had instead been crushed where they stood by the backhoes into heaps of timbers, broken window sashes, bent doors and twisted tin eaves. Dwight stopped in front of where his own home had been. A gouge of earth.

He shouldered a daypack with a bottle of water and few sundries, donned a flat-brimmed farmer's straw hat he had had for decades and made his way to the festivities.

When he got to the field the first person he saw was Darcy. He was crouched at one end of the space, surrounded by half a dozen onlookers — four children and two adults. He was using a large folding knife that he carried on his belt to whittle at a club-like piece of cottonwood. The bark had been stripped, and he was working to taper it at one end.

Bro, Darcy said. The man of the hour. This is my brother, he said to the boy standing near. The guy I was telling you about. Born right here.

What are you doing here, Dwight said. He was standing just outside of Darcy's circle.

Baseball, Darcy said. We're having a ball game in your honour.

Were you really born right here, a boy said.

Look at this, Darcy said. I made a bat. He hefted himself to a standing position. Stand back boys and girls, he said. But he barely waited long enough for them to clear a space when he began taking cuts with the homemade bat. One of the boys flinched and hit the dirt.

You shouldn't be here, Dwight said. He couldn't get a look at Darcy's eyes. They were shrouded behind a pair of sunglasses. But he was willing to lay short odds that he was high. Tweaking, or buzzing on coke. He was wearing a black Ozzy! T-shirt. Sweat stained the shirt blacker in arcs under the arms and down the back.

Hey, Justin, Darcy called to one of the dreadlockians who was beating down the grass with a shovel to clear a basepath. Where's that ball? Darcy said.

Dude, I keep telling you, it's *Jordan*, Jordan said.

Jordan, Justin, Jason. Whatever man, Darcy said. Pitch me that ball. Jordan dropped his shovel and trotted to where the brush had been tramped down to define the pitcher's mound. Not exactly a mound. A circle. Jordan picked up a lumpy looking spheroid of wood. Darcy had carved a ball of sorts. Jordan lofted it to Darcy, but it dropped six feet short.

C'mon man, Darcy said. Give it some English. He turned to the boy who had flinched, but who was now standing. Hey kid, give it a try. The boy was maybe twelve, a good size for his age, wholesome looking. He was wearing a T-shirt that said Hug a Tree Today, safari-type shorts and good quality hiking boots. One of the adults, a man in his forties, cleared his throat as if to prepare to speak. Darcy cut the man off with a wave of his hand, grinned wide to show his gappy teeth. It's cool, man. The boy looked at the adult who was no doubt his father, received some sort of invisible signal, and fetched the wooden ball. He bounded to the pitcher's mound. The boy delivered a textbook slo-pitch throw, so it arrived right at Darcy's beltline. Darcy cut at the ball with a beautiful upward swing, transferring his weight to his forward foot as he pulled the bat, swivelling his hips to face the ball. His ample belly swerved too, and all the force of his motion and weight funnelled down his arms and into the moving bat. The club met the ball with a satisfying crack and launched it into the air. He followed through with the bat held high over his left shoulder as if it were a twig. The ball sailed toward centre-right in a high looping arc, well past the baseline. If a fielder had been there, he or she would have had to turn and run toward the fences, if fences had been there. As the ball began to descend from its zenith, the father of the pitcher had the presence of mind to yell, Fore! The SmarTec consultants looked over, but didn't have time to sort out what was happening before the wooden projectile arrived where they were. It missed them, but hit their barbecue, making a sound like a ringing bell, then bounced and hit the side of the truck.

Yeah, Darcy said. He fist pumped the air. Home run. And I hit the bastard's truck. Let's play ball, Darcy hollered.

Wow, the pitcher said.

Dude, Jordan and Jared said.

The pitcher and the other kids set off in a gamboling rush of knees and sneakers to fetch the ball, which had been picked up by one of the security guards.

How did you get here, Dwight said.

Man, you got to stop with all these questions, Darcy said, turning to point the bat at his brother. I am here. This is a free country. Deal with it.

How is Amy about all this, Dwight said. How's Willow.

There you go again, man, Darcy said. Those fucking questions. His grin had slipped. The fucking third degree. Darcy cast an imploring look to the father of the pitcher, who was still standing there. Can you believe this guy, he said to the man. He's my brother, and for our whole fucking life he's at me with questions all the time. Darcy made a talking gesture with his free hand. Beak beak beak, he said. You're always fucking beaking at me.

Um, maybe you can watch your language, the man said. The kids and all.

Do you see any kids here, right fucking now, Darcy said. I watched my mouth when those rug rats were around but they aren't here. I'm talking to my fucking brother now. So fuck off.

The man looked like he might say something, thought better of it, and turned and walked to where the kids were playing catch in the outfield.

You want some fucking answers. OK here's some answers. I'm here 'cause this is where I'm from, just like you, dipshit. I got here with that fucking vanload of lesbians who are shooting that fucking film. And I brought a fucking PA system. That's right, wiseass, I gave them the fucking money they needed, so fuck off. I didn't talk to Amy. She looked at me like I was a turd on her shoe and turned her fucking back. Willow came over to me and gave me a hug. And now you. Is that enough fucking answers for one afternoon?

I just—, Dwight said. He couldn't finish the thought. Darcy walked away, beating the grass with the bat as he went. He gathered Jordan and Jared. The three of them walked off into the bush. Going to get high, Dwight thought.

As he walked toward the literature table, a voice called his name: Mr. Eliot. Smithson. The two men faced each other. Smithson leaned on a cane.

Hello, Mr. Smithson, Dwight said. Smithson was wearing a beige poplin windbreaker, khakis, and a golf visor. Bits of hair wisped in the breeze. He seemed a shade of the gentrified cowboy of ten years ago.

How's your nose, Smithson said. His speech was slurred, the corner on the left side of his mouth turned down.

Crooked, Dwight said. How's yours.

Clean, Smithson said. Not sure I can say the same for your brother. He flicked his eyes briefly to where Darcy and the Js had been.

Am I my brother's keeper? Dwight said.

Touché and cliché, Mr. Eliot, Smithson said. Although I think you are twisting Cain's words. Seems to me the point the scriptures are trying to make is that indeed we are our brothers' keepers. As he spoke Darcy, Jordan, and Jared emerged from the bushes and walked towards the water table. If Darcy saw them, if he recognized Smithson, he showed no sign. I suppose you want an apology, Smithson said.

Boadicea began to bark. Dwight watched as the dog chased the wooden ball and snatched it away from the children in the outfield. Never asked for one, Dwight said. This — he touched the bridge of his nose — was just collateral damage.

My only regret is that I didn't smash your brother's face, too, Smithson said. Or worse.

Well, today's your chance, Dwight said.

The spirit is willing, but the flesh is weak, if I may continue with our biblical allusions, Smithson said. He gestured with his cane, as if to register his infirmity. My turn to twist meaning. I don't think Matthew had assault and battery in mind. They fell silent again. Boadicea barked. A child cried. Are you going to ask about Sara.

OK. How's Sara, Dwight said.

She's fine. Her nose is clean, too, Smithson said. Married. Kids. She's in Toronto.

And Molly, Dwight said.

Dead, Smithson said.

I'm sorry, Dwight said.

I am too, Smithson said. Amy had control of Boadicea now, and wrested the ball away. Simon Love gestured and she tossed it to him.

I don't think I want to make small talk, Mr. Smithson, Dwight said.

Understandable, Smithson said. It has never been my forte, either. The two men watched as Simon Love joined the kids in the field and played catch. Look at him, Dwight said. Just playing at being a regular guy.

I once told you, Mr. Eliot, that I am a man of not inconsiderable means. I despise that man, Smithson said, nodding towards Love. I support what you and Ms. Howse are trying to achieve here. Men like Mr. Love have limited imaginations. They will not be satisfied until the whole valley from Calgary to Banff is converted into a vast shopping mall and condominium complex. That is all they can imagine. What do you imagine, Mr. Eliot?

They stood in the field where Dwight was born. Dwight tried to imagine all the men he had been or could be, all at the same time. A boy clutching a bloodied stick. The scrape of a razor on his neck. He was driving a car. He was tossing chips on a roulette table. He was a bubblegum-pink baby freshly deposited in Laugh Jack's hands. He was here, now.

Nothing, Dwight said. This. The blue dome. Grasshoppers. The faint white noise of the water rushing through the spillway of the dam.

Walk me to my car, Smithson said. They moved across the space, Smithson stiff-legged and slow, probing with his cane when the ground appeared uncertain or uneven. When they got to the road and neared the Lincoln that Smithson pointed to, Simon Love approached.

Smithson, Love said. He held out his hand.

Simon, Smithson said. He didn't look up, nor lift his hand from the cane to extend his own.

It's good to see you out and about, Love said. We've been worried about you.

We, Smithson said. We, whom. He had his car-key fob in his good hand now, and pressed the remote lock. He looked at Love. I didn't realize you were plural.

This is just business, Smithson, Love said. No need to get personal.

My business is always personal, Smithson said. Just ask Dwight, here. He can tell you. He opened the door and negotiated his rigid body into the driver's seat. We'll be in touch, he said, in a way that made it unclear if he addressed Dwight, Love, or both. Smithson pulled away, gunning the accelerator slightly to spray a little gravel.

People began to assemble for the parade. At the head, a group calling themselves "Puppets for Change" drew the crowd. They had huge fabric and papier mâché figures on poles: representations of an eagle, a First Nations Chief, a giant tree, blue jays with twelve-foot wingspans, wildflowers, a life-size moose. One person walked on stilts, with a coyote head hoisted on her shoulders. Another on stilts had the head of a cat, and sported a padded bodysuit tented with a pinstripe suit. A sash across the chest proclaimed: Capitalist Fat Cat. They passed out red foam rubber orbs that could be clapped on a face to make a clown nose.

As the parade began to snake its way along the road toward the teepee and then the dam, a woman at the front of the line made a squelch with a bullhorn, then found the right button. She began to lead chants:

When I say development, you say: No Way! she called.

Development, she called.

No way, the crowd responded, with spotty enthusiasm.

Development.

No way. Louder.

Development.

No way! Louder still.

At the edge, a TV crew followed along. The filmmakers were right in the thick of things, with two handheld high-definition cameras and a sound team with a boom mic. The chants changed:

How do you want your water? the bullhorn led.

Fresh!

When do you want it?

Forever!

The heat of the afternoon began to take its toll. Several families with children hived off from the march and made their way back to the field, where they took shade under the trees and passed around bottles of water. The children put their clown noses on and off. The chanting became more ragged, then petered out. The fat cat stiltwalker stepped in a gopher hole and fell slowly and awkwardly into a rainbow banner. The TV crew tried to sneak off, and Willow went after them, imploring them to stay for the speeches. The parade leaders responded by cutting the route short, abandoning the walk through the blasted townsite to return to the centre of the gathering. Jordan, Jared, and Darcy had brought four folding tables together over by the earthmoving equipment to make a stage, and set up the PA. A few words had been exchanged with the corporate security detail, but Simon Love had disembarked from the air-conditioned cool of his Cadillac and given his blessing. The two Js and Darcy snaked an extension cord behind the idle bulldozers and fired up the portable generator to power the amps. Throughout the speeches the murmur of the internal combustion engine provided an insistent soundtrack.

It made for good TV, with the giant yellow machines looming in the background, and puppets in the foreground, as the organizers made their appeals. Willow acted as emcee. First she acknowledged that they were all on traditional First Nations territory—inhabited for centuries, then negotiated as treaty land, then ceded, and now in transition. But, she said, ownership is fleeting. She called on everyone present to honour and respect the traditions and people whose guests they were— whether here at Seep or anywhere on Turtle Island.

We are not in opposition to this change for the sake of opposition, Willow concluded. We are here to question whether change for the sake of change can sustain us — sustain us here, at Seep, and sustain us here, on earth. It is time to ask what we can do, as a community, as a people, as human beings, men, women, and children, to make a better world. And maybe this time, a better world can be made by resisting change for change's sake.

Others got up to say a few words, but in the swelter of the day, after an afternoon in the field, they kept their speeches short. A representative of the dissenting group from the band talked about the opportunity to reclaim a land that had been stolen and used to make money; and now they had the chance to let the land be the land, but had been seduced by the allure of making more money. The water-advocacy speaker warned that the Bow watershed had limits on development, that the Bow was already a dangerously overburdened resource. When it seemed the last speech was done, and Willow was beginning to urge folks to stick around for the games and the barbecue and the lantern festival (a group of volunteers had been busy making jam-jar lanterns all day), Darcy clambered awkwardly onto the makeshift stage. He looked a little unsteady on his feet, but then got his bearings. He grabbed Willow in a bear hug, cutting her off, then took the microphone from her hand.

Good afternoon, Seep lovers, he said. Some people clapped, as if they were unsure of the appropriate way to respond. Another organizer came over but Willow gestured it was OK. Dwight moved his way forward.

Isn't she something, Darcy said, resting the mic against his chin like a pro. Can you believe this is my daughter? Can you believe it? He gathered Willow with his free arm. The crowd applauded. They liked Willow. Maybe this fat biker-looking guy was OK.

Can I say, you won't believe this, Darcy said. But this is my hometown. His voice rose in volume, and elicited some cheers. Oh, hey. I forgot. He reached into a pocket for something, then donned a clown nose. That's better, eh? More cheering. The TV crew, who had set up over by Simon Love's Escalade to interview him, hastily jogged over to catch what could prove to be the unscripted moment.

OK, let's get down and dirty, Darcy said. What's going on here, it's stupid. S-T-U-pid. All these bulldozers and shit. Does this valley really need more condos? A smattering of Nos! and No ways! from the crowd. No, it's just stupid. Hey. You see this lunkhead? He pointed to Dwight, who was at the edge of table-cum-stage. This is my little bro. Willow's uncle. A few more cheers. And this guy was born right here. Darcy paused, then roared into the mic: I mean *right here*. Our mother gave birth to this little fu— , oops. He clapped a hand to his mouth. This little shit was born right over there in the middle of a goddamned riot. A baseball riot. Right on this very spot. On this very field. Fifty years ago this weekend, right little bro?

Darcy, Dwight said. Cut it out. Dwight was reaching up now, as if he could catch Darcy if the older brother jumped.

You wanna tell the story, bro, Darcy said. Dwight shook his head, reached for the mic cord. Naw, he's too shy, Darcy said. And the truth is, it's a long and boring story, and I heard it about a thousand times, so I ain't gonna tell it either. But here's what we're gonna do. Let's sing him Happy Birthday. C'mon. Darcy began to sing, with surprising timbre and pitch, and by the second line many had joined in. At the end of the last line, spontaneous hoots and hollers. All right, Darcy said. Now. In honour of this little s.o.b. coming into the world right here, we're gonna have ourselves a baseball game. Our own baseball riot. So come on everybody, let's stop building shit around here and play ball. He dropped the mic to his side, then raised it again. And then let's eat some chow. He struck a rock-star pose, clown nose and all, mic held in the air. Then he twirled it Daltrey-style, barely missing Willow and hitting the stage, sending an amplified *clunk!* through the crowd. He dangled the mic over the speaker and a feedback whine started slowly, then accelerated into a sudden howl. He popped it up like a yoyo in his hand. I said, let's play ball. The crowd was dispersing. He tossed the mic to the table where it cracked through the PA and he jumped to the ground, almost falling, catching himself with two quick hops.

They did play ball. Enough volunteers stepped forward to fill out two teams. Each side fielded ten players, with the extras filling in holes in the outfield and in the infield. They managed to make do with about half the original ball diamond, but still contended with alders, willows, and the rusting vehicle chassis. The bases were marked with jackets tossed at paced-off intervals. No one had a glove — What has happened to kids these days that they don't come to a picnic with an effing ball glove, Darcy roared. Someone found a pair of ski mitts in a car so at least the first base and catcher had some protection. The homemade bat and ball were serviceable. Flies were dropped, throws to first went wild, grounders were booted. Darcy proclaimed himself umpire, but also took a turn at bat whenever the bases were loaded. He hit a homer every time. They made it through the batting order for each team three or four times before the homemade ball broke in half on a sharp grounder. The shortstop threw one half to first, and the third base used the other half to tag a runner. Double play, called Darcy. Game called on account of a broken ball.

A few of the non-players had come over to talk to Dwight about his story. The filmmakers were particularly interested, especially when he began to reveal all he knew about the way the townsite had been made and remade, used and reused. And the TV asked him for a sound bite.

There's no way they can bring the town back, Dwight said. I mean they took all the houses away. But this new scheme. They'll just want to tear it all down again in a few years. Build it up, tear it down. It makes no sense.

Can you put a nose on, like your brother did? one of the TV producers asked.

No, Dwight said.

They ate. The ranchers served beef and beans. The organic market served tofu. Salads were consumed. Pies were sliced and eaten. Watermelons carved. As the dusk began to settle, some of the folks, especially those with younger children, packed up and made their way home. The cowboys trailered their horses and headed out. The drumming started again by the teepee. The RCMP departed. Some who remained cracked beers. The contracted security guards allowed a bonfire to happen at second base. Volunteers scrounged wood from the demolished houses. Darcy took it upon himself to be Fire Master, fetching a jerry can of gasoline used to service the portable generator. The lantern people gathered the decorated jam-jars and deployed the tea lights, readying them for sunset. Dwight found himself at the fire, and was surprised that Simon Love had come over to stand beside him.

Well, Mr. Andersson, Simon Love said. Jon with no h.

Mr. Love, Dwight said.

It was a fine day here, Love said.

Don't mock this, Dwight said.

I'm not mocking, Love said. I am impressed with the passion. The passion for place.

Really.

Yes, really, Love said. You might find this hard to fathom, but I'm passionate about this place too.

About the money you can make, Dwight said.

That's part of it, Love said. But I can make more money in easier places. Love was charring the end of a piece of deadfall cottonwood in the fire. No, I mean it. I know this is a special place. I guess the way I figure it, I've got a plan so others can enjoy it.

Hmm. Dwight said. They watched for a few minutes in silence as the lanterns were lit, and people picked them up. Each jar was attached with twists of wire to a bamboo stick. The puppets too were lit from within and hoisted on their poles.

You can't hold up progress, Love said. We're going to do this.

I know, Dwight said.

Just then, the PA crackled to life. An electric guitar power chord ripped through the evening quiet. In the lull, as the ringing notes subsided, the gentle purr of the generator hummed. Another power chord. Suddenly, with a whoosh, one of the porta-potties burst into flame. The smell of gasoline wafted in the air, joined shortly by the smell of burning plastics. Another power chord, and Darcy's gravelly voice:

Ladies and Gentlemen! On your feet or on your knees for rock and roll!

Another porta-potty leapt alight. In the glow of the flames, there was Darcy, still with the red nose but now without a shirt, as he began to crash out riffs on the guitar, singing along raggedly. *Yeah Yeah Hey Hey. Rock and roll is here to stay.* The contracted security guards approached him, but out of the shadows Jordan and Jared appeared, holding their spades like staves, flanking Darcy on either side. They had red clown noses too. The guards hesitated. Love was already on his cellphone, talking to the RCMP. Amy emerged, with Boadicea bounding beside her.

Dwight could hear her cursing Darcy: You fucking stupid shit. As she approached, Jared stepped forward, menacing her with his shovel. Amy stood her ground. Jared pushed the spade towards her at cross arms, more as a warning than as an assault. She grabbed the haft of the tool in both her hands and pushed back. He staggered, and the two of them pushed and pulled at each other. Amy wouldn't go down. She was small but squat, built low to the ground. Jared tried to kick at her. Locked as they both were to the handle of the shovel, he lost his balance. Amy twisted the shaft and the two of them fell to the ground. Boadicea became frantic and started snapping. People were running for their cars. Smouldering lanterns littered the ground where they had been dropped. A blue jay puppet caught fire and tried to launch itself in an uprush of heated air. Then a moose burst into flames. Behind Darcy, one by one, the bulldozers, graders, excavators and backhoes began to burn. And still he played, crashing out classic rock chords. One of the other guards came running to the fracas. Jordan cracked his spade over the man's knee, dropping him. Boadicea turned and lunged at Jordan, teeth bared. The young man swung and clanged the dog on the skull with the head of the spade. She went down without a whimper. The generator caught fire. The PA went dead. Darcy unslung the silenced guitar and began to wield it like a battle-axe. He slashed at the security guards who were trying to corner him. He backed up toward the inferno behind.

Dwight hung back, watching. Willow was with her mother who was now sitting up, cradling her dog. Two security people laid their boots into Jared, who curled on the ground trying to protect his head.

Jordan was still holding off a guard with his shovel. And the flames went higher.

An RCMP SUV arrived. The road was blocked with people in their cars trying to flee. The police vehicle crashed through the underbrush, bounced over ditches, flattened willows and alders, and roared into the field. The police officers jumped out. They approached Darcy, who was still swinging the guitar. The security guards saw the police and re-treated. Jared was on the ground, handcuffed. Jordan dropped his shovel and raised his hands.

You're too late, pigs, Jordan said. We got these motherfuckers. Amy was on her feet now. She ran at Jordan, tackling him at the waist. She got a handful of dreadlock and drove her forehead into his face. Then she began to rain punches on him.

You killed my dog, she yelled. The police ran to her and tried to pull her off. One of them pinned her arms behind her back and pulled. Mom! Willow screamed. She's not dead, she's waking up. Darcy charged, swinging the guitar. He connected solidly with the officer's back. She let go of Amy and rolled away. Jordan lay on the ground, bleeding from his face. Darcy and the other police officer faced each other. Darcy had the guitar poised over his head, the police officer had a hand on his still-holstered gun. Drop it! the cop said. The police officer who had been hit by Darcy lurched to her feet and drew her conducted energy device. She fired the taser and its probes latched onto Darcy's bare chest.

Darcy dropped the guitar. His muscles tensed, the cords on his neck stood out, his hands curled. He keeled over. He tried to get up and the officer fired another pulse. The second officer fired his taser. Darcy began to twitch, arching his back in a kind of wrestler's bridge. His tongue lolled out of his mouth. Now Dwight had come forward. The police officers rolled Darcy on his front and put him in handcuffs. Darcy! Dwight called. He could see Darcy's eyes were rolled up; his swollen tongue protruded as if flexed, pointing into the earth. His face was ashen. And still the fires.

He's not breathing! Dwight yelled. One of the police officers held her knee on Darcy's neck while the other searched his pockets. Dwight could see that Darcy's hands were blackened with soot and he could smell gasoline. The searching officer pulled a crack stem from Darcy's pants. He reached inside his protective vest and found an evidence bag.

He's not breathing! Dwight yelled again. He's fucking dying! They moved Darcy onto his back. His spine was still arched. His eyes were open. He wasn't breathing. Two more RCMP units had arrived. Two of the reinforcements relieved the officers of Darcy. They began CPR, even though Darcy was still handcuffed, his arms behind his back, as they tried to perform chest compressions.

Take the fucking cuffs off! Dwight screamed. He felt a hand on his arm, he threw it off, ready to punch whoever it was, until he saw it was Bill, the man he had met yesterday at the roulette table.

It's OK son, Bill said. Don't get yourself killed too.

This is my letter to you.

Love, your mother.

18.

Bolide

8 August 2009

From the west what started as a white streak became brighter, and zoomed its way eastward. The sky lit up like daytime, matching with its brightness the fire raging on the ground. Everyone who could still see looked up. The cops doing CPR, Jordan and Jared, Willow, Amy, Dwight. Simon Love, Bill and Beth. The film crew, the security guards. Those in the cars leaving the site, those in Caxton, in Malcolm, in Calgary. Cows on farms lifted their heads. Coyotes paused in their tracks. As it passed overhead it flared, once, then again, then burst and faded as it travelled eastward. And the night swallowed the light. It had lasted perhaps five seconds, a handful of heartbeats, for those whose hearts were still beating.

I'll be damned, Bill said. A goddamned bolide. Did you see that, Beth? The man turned to find his wife. A bolide.

Dwight looked at his brother. Darcy had not seen the fireball. Darcy was dead.

00.

"Amy's" Coda

22 August 2009

So here it is: the last word. I get it. Me, "Amy Howse," daughter of "Beulah." Whose father is — well, Beulah was never entirely clear on that. The birth certificate says "Father: Wayne 'Howse.'" He was mom's husband but was long gone before she had me. Very long gone — like before nine months long gone. Before you start thinking that there must be a trick ending here — Aha! Her dad was Dwight's dad! They were half-siblings! — I'll stop you there. I was born in the city, during the years my mother was living there. Her mother, my grandmother, left the reserve with her white husband. And then my mom was born in the city and grew up and had her own white husband. And then she moved back to Seep with me. She came back when I was a month old, moved into the little trailer in the no man's land past the yard where they stored power poles. Squeezed between the reserve, railway tracks and town. "Illegal housing units," as they might say nowadays. The yard foreman Graeme Meehan stuck three trailers and built three shacks on a piece of dirt that belonged to the railway or the power company or somebody. Or nobody. My mom was the most permanent resident. The other places were rented out to women like my mom, who had lost their reserve status and their husbands, or to itinerant workers — some of the ballplayers back in those days, labourers on the dam or guys stringing wires, highway crews. He even tried one summer to get a clientele of city folk, called the three shacks "cabins" and decorated them like Swiss getaways, with red eaves and geranium pots, built bunk beds and put in hide-a-beds. He called it the Seep Shangri-La Chalets. But most folks called us Dogpatch — Li'l Abner was still in the papers then. Or the Seep Ozarks. Or other things.

I don't know how much to believe about the stories that are in these pages. Some of it is true. I had a little dog that disappeared when I was eleven years old. We blamed it on the coyotes. If his story here is to be believed, I guess he and "Darcy" killed it. Some of it is made-up. I like to think that part about the little dog is made-up. I still have Boadicea. She never got clobbered. And some of it I just don't know if it's made-up or not.

I never knew about his gambling — or at least how bad it was. Along with the box of these pages, he also left a brown envelope with $40,000 cash, and the keys to his house in the city. So maybe the money hidden under the deck was real. "Willow" never saw it. She had a visit with her dad at "Dwight's" place in June, they sat on a newly built deck. But no one had a bag of cash. The "Dwight" I knew did see his house on the highway. He was born during a baseball riot. There are developers who are working hard to turn our old company town and some of the reserve land into a resort. There have been protests. There was never a picnic. Some construction equipment was burned. Last weekend, in the middle of the night, two bulldozers, a backhoe and a company truck — my company truck — went up in flames. Same night the box of papers showed up in my doghouse. I think the developers are happy with the fire. The economy's gone into the tank, so it gives them an excuse to stop work. Somebody's going to collect a big insurance payout for the fire. Maybe they did it themselves.

His brother "Darcy" did die in police custody after being tasered. That happened a couple of months ago. In the city, outside a bar. A fight, a knife, drugs. They're calling it "excited delirium." They always call it excited delirium — it has nothing to do with the fact that they just juiced several thousands volts into some guy — he had excited delirium! Who knew? "Darcy" had spent a lot of time in prison — or the pen, as he was quick to call it, if you accidentally said "jail." One shouldn't speak ill of the dead, but what the hell. He was a charming, exhausting, manipulative, deceitful prick, and in this case he might be better off dead. And the world too. I didn't go to the funeral. I think it was just Dwight and his mom. Maybe that's why his mom spilled the beans about his dad. The real Dwight's mom could talk just fine, still had her jaw and voicebox. She's not in a nursing home — she has a cozy little condo in Malcolm. She can talk, but she hardly ever does.

So I grew up in "Seep" and I'm still here, though not for long. Seep — or the town I live in that Seep resembles — is almost gone. In "Dwight's" story, there is an "old town," and a "new town," but my version of Seep, the real one, only has one side, and it was and is company-owned. Now that the work here has ground to a halt, I have to move out of the ATCO trailer that I've been living in as part of the security detail.

The house I grew up in — Beulah's trailer — was where Stitch Washington tried to hide from the Cubans. Don't believe that crap about my mom being a hostage. Bullshit. That's what my mom used to call it: bullshit. She could never remember Stitch's name. He lived in one of the shacks, and spent some time in the trailer, along with other men. I was living with granny-aunt on the reserve for those first years, until my mother got sober when I was three or four. She never gave out a lot of details, but she would only say that hers was "a house of ill repute." Then she'd laugh like hell.

The newspaper that Dwight showed me once, and the stories that got told, usually said that some Cubans crashed into our house, held a knife to my mom's throat, and generally threatened harm. But she was firm — "that coward n-word clobbered the Mexican and tried to run home." His shack was the second one over from the trailer. Stitch ran fast, and he figured his chasers would give up. But they didn't. So when he got to Dogpatch, he ran to mom's because they were gaining on him. Yes, he grabbed a knife. And yes, it's true that when Graeme Meehan saw the Cubans beating on the trailer with baseball bats, he came over with a .22. And Dwight's dad showed up with half the men from the town and helped settle things down. But as my mom would say, "It was a white man's thing. They were arguing about money." And then she'd laugh like hell.

Here's the thing: I forgive Dwight. I forgive him if he killed my dog when he was ten years old. I forgive him for never trying to date me. Instead I got stuck with that bastard brother of his. Him I don't forgive, dead or not.

I knew Dwight was sweet on me going to school. The way he was so sarcastic. And scared of me. I guess he was feeling like he had betrayed me or something, killing my dog. And when I dropped out and got a little wild, I think I ended up with Darcy because I knew Dwight liked me. Of course I ended up with a lot of guys for a while. Then back to Darcy. I got Willow out of that scumbag. For her sake, I'm lucky he never stayed.

Where am I going with all this? I forgive Dwight. I forgive him for the sarcasm. For getting me fired from my job. Damn, if those machines didn't look good burning in the night.

But I don't forgive him for disappearing. Darcy disappears. Dwight — well, he goes away for long periods, but he doesn't disappear.

Without "Dwight," there is no ending. I will wait for him, for when I can see him again. He will walk up to me in ten years. I'll be standing on the shiny new street of the new "New Seep" or whatever they will call it, maybe in front of a Starbucks, or on the small green space of a condominium lawn, where I will be wearing a sandwich board that will either say "Eat Free @ The Casino" or "Save the Wilderness, Sell Your House." Or maybe, if the economy doesn't pick up, I'll be standing in an overgrown scrub of land where the prairie meets mountain under a porridge sky, playing fetch with my dog. And he will look me in the eye, and say, Hi Amy.

I will look at him and say, Hi Dwight, long time no see.

Acknowledgements

I have had some very astute readers who helped shape my vision. I am especially indebted to Aritha van Herk for her patience, guidance, and acumen, and her faith in this project. Tom Wayman never let me off the hook, and helped me understand my own writing. Warren Cariou, Pamela McCallum, and Dianne Draper offered insightful readings. My former colleague Chris Frey has been an invaluable asker of necessary questions and giver of sage advice. Conversations with Susan Swan about the nature of narrative happened at a critical time in the development of this novel — thank you, Susan.

A big thanks to Anvil Press: Brian Kaufman and Karen Green and Shazia Hafiz Ramji. You guys are awesome.

Thank you Levente Kovacs, for creating the planning illustration. All rights for the illustration are held by W. Mark Giles. The photograph, *Site of Proposed Horseshoe Dam, 1907*, is courtesy of the Glenbow Archives, NA-4416-7. Used by permission under licence.

Thank you to Rae Sharpe for logistical support that helped me manage time and resources. And I am forever appreciative of the staff and facilities at the Banff Centre.

I acknowledge the financial support of The Killam Trusts, The Social Sciences and Humanities Research Council of Canada, and The University of Calgary.

I am grateful to have shared the experience and stories of growing up in a small town with my large group of siblings: Laurie, Susan, Michael, Nancy, Pat, Aurelian, and Dean — you have all helped make this story in ways great and subtle. And I am indebted to the frequent storytelling of my late mother, Secord Giles (née Jackson).

I owe so much to Donna Sharpe: I thank you from the bottom of my heart. And finally, to Lucy Piper Giles Sharpe — you teach me so much.

After many years mired in the middle-management muddle of transnational corporations, Mark is now a writer and an educator. His first book *Knucklehead & Other Stories* (Anvil Press) was honoured with the W.O. Mitchell City of Calgary Book Award. His writing — fiction, poetry, and non-fiction — has appeared in magazines in both Canada and the U.S.A. Saskatchewan-born, Edmonton-raised, with stops in Victoria, Kelowna, Montreal, and Halifax, W. Mark Giles now calls Calgary home.